E.T.
THE EXTRA-TERRESTRIAL

THE MOVIE

D0067954

SIMON SPOTLIGHT
An imprint of Simon & Schuster Children's Publishing Division
1230 Avenue of the Americas, New York, New York 10020

Manufactured in the United States of America

First Edition
2 4 6 8 10 9 7 5 3 1

ISBN 0-689-84367-4

E.T.
THE EXTRA-TERRESTRIAL

THE MOVIE

adapted by Terry Collins

based on a motion picture screenplay by
Melissa Mathison

Simon Spotlight

New York   London   Toronto   Sydney   Singapore

CHAPTER 1

The sky turned from day to night, and one by one by one, stars began to poke through, twinkling over the shadowy forest below.

On this night, though, one of the stars came closer, and as it fell, there was no sound, not even when it landed. A spaceship now stood among the trees. The ship was not large, nor did it come with fins and speed jets like old-fashioned rocket ships. More than anything, it looked like a hot-air balloon filled with a million dancing fireflies.

A round door opened on the ship and pink light spilled out. A ramp lowered, and a group of strange creatures slowly waddled down it. The beings were short with long, skinny arms.

In their chests glowed red "heart-lights." They seemed to use them to speak to each other without words.

As the creatures walked out, they made soft cooing sounds as they looked at the beautiful landscape. Using a variety of tools that looked like small shovels, sticks, and pails, they collected plant and soil samples to take back to their ship.

This would be the last mission to Earth for a very long time.

The ship flickered behind them as one of the alien creatures moved away from the others, going deeper into the woods searching for new plants. The gigantic redwood trees made the visitor's body seem even smaller as he looked down, stepping carefully around the wild flowers. Every once in a while, he used his long fingers to dig, pull, and then knock the soil off the roots of a plant.

A rabbit turned to watch the creature with no fear. All was quiet, except for the crickets, the water in the nearby stream, and the creature's soft breathing.

Suddenly a truck with blinding headlights roared past the alien. He froze, and instantly his heart-light flashed a warning red, glowing through his chest. Closer to the ship other heart-lights flashed red too.

Back at the redwoods more trucks pulled up blocking the creature from his ship. Men leapt out of their trucks, leaving the engines running and the headlights on as they searched the area with flashlights. A man with a huge ring of keys jingling from his belt loop took the lead, gesturing the others forward.

The creature ran from the men, trying to make it to his ship without being seen. His heart-light glowed and his feet snapped twigs as he ran. The man with the keys heard the sounds and shined his flashlight on the spot where the alien had been standing. The bushes still shook. Because he was so scared, the creature seemed to almost glide along the forest floor.

More men carrying flashlights reached the edge of the clearing, shielding their eyes from the white light as the spacecraft rose. Behind the humans a single red heart-light glowed.

A man noticed the shimmering red glow and called out to the group, pointing to it. The creature looked up as he ran from them, his eyes shining with fear as he watched his ship disappear into the sky.

He moaned sadly. The creature, an extra-terrestrial, was now stranded on Earth.

One of the men shined his flashlight on the alien again. The alien ran to the outer reaches of the forest and looked out over the slope upon a patchwork of lights below. There, in the distant valley, was the city.

He looked around and could see the men coming closer. The woods were no longer safe, so he found his way slowly down the hill toward the city, leaving the men with the flashlights following his tracks to the rocky slope.

CHAPTER 2

What had looked like a kitchen table a few hours ago was now a mess of soda bottles, potato chip bags, reference books, sheets of notebook paper, pocket calculators, pencils, and tiny metal figurines. A game of Dungeons & Dragons was in progress.

Steve, a tall, skinny boy with glasses, looked at the game book. "Okay, so you've been followed out of the forest by a herd of goblins . . ."

"How many?" Michael said, wrinkling his freckled nose.

"Ten," Steve replied.

Michael frowned. "How close are they?"

"They are *on* you," Steve said flatly. "Who's in the lead here?"

"Me," Michael answered. "Well, my magic user."

"Goblin rolls," Steve announced, picking up a die and rolling it across the cluttered tabletop.

"This is dumb. I'm ordering a pizza," Tyler mumbled, getting up and grabbing the phone receiver off the kitchen wall.

"Goblin One shoots his crossbow and . . . sixteen! He hits!"

"Roll damage?" Michael asked.

"One arrow in the chest. You're out for ten melee rounds," Steve said with relish.

"I've got resurrection, Mike. I'll bring you back," Greg said.

Michael shot Greg a look. "I'm already one of the undead, stupid. Hey, Steve . . . I can still throw spells, right?"

"How about throwing a spell over to Pizza Man while you're at it," Tyler said. "Where's our pizza, man? Get it?"

Across the room, separated by the kitchen counter from the teenage boys, Michael's younger brother, Elliott, peered down at a tiny metal figure. His dark eyes were lost in a past time of knights, dragons, goblins, and dungeons.

"Okay, then," Elliott said softly, pushing his hair out of his eyes as he plotted his plan of action. "So I run out of the forest, and I think I'll shoot just my arrows at the goblins to make them chase me. I keep running and shooting and running and shooting, and just when they're really mad and about to get me, I throw down my portable hole and climb in and pull the lid closed. Presto! Vanished."

The older boys continued the game.

"You guys, I'm ready to play now," a frustrated Elliott yelled.

Greg rolled his eyes. "We're in the middle of the game, Elliott. You can't just enter the universe in the middle."

"Mike?" Elliott asked again.

Michael shrugged. "You'll have to ask Steve. He's the Game Master. He's got absolute power."

Steve pointed at the figure in Elliott's hand. "Okay. What have you got?" he asked.

Elliott held up the pewter figure proudly. "Elf. First class."

The older boys cracked up with laughter.

"Elliott!" A new voice called, female, older, and annoyed: his mother.

A grinning Steve nodded toward Elliott's pewter elf. "Is he land, hill, or aquatic?"

"Elliott!" His mother called again, louder this time.

"You'd better go see what Mom wants," Michael warned.

Elliott began to back out of the kitchen. "Come on, Steve," Elliott pleaded. "Let me play."

"For you, Elliott, I'll make an exception. But first—"

"ELLIOTT!"

"You go wait for the pizza," Tyler said, waving the cash for the deliveryman under Elliott's nose.

"Then I'm in?"

"In," Steve replied.

Elliott snatched the money and ran out of the kitchen, heading upstairs before his mother's yelling brought the ceiling down.

"Yeah, Mom?" Elliott asked, stepping into his bedroom.

His mother's back was to him as she finished tucking in the bedspread of the top bunk. "What do you see?" she asked.

Elliott shrugged. "I dunno."

Mary turned to her son. She was already in her robe, ready to go to bed. "Do you see what this room looks like right now?"

Elliott looked. He could see the carpet, which was rare since he usually kept most of his clothing and toys in piles on the floor.

"Clean," he said.

"Brand-*new* clean," Mary said. "No dirty dishes. Clothes put away. Beds made. Desk neat."

"Thanks," Elliott said, and he meant it.

Mary didn't reply as she reached down and picked up a letter from Elliott's desk. She looked down at the envelope and looked up again.

"This is what a mature person's room is supposed to look like," Mary said. "All of the time."

"I know," said Elliott.

She looked again at the return address on the envelope, again at the name.

"What did your father have to say?" she asked, keeping her tone casual.

"Oh, nothing."

"In the letter, did he mention you guys coming to visit?"

"Thanksgiving."

"Thanksgiving? I want Thanksgiving!" Mary exclaimed.

She dropped the envelope back on the desk and scanned her eyes over the walls. "Um, you want to repaint in here?" she said, changing the subject. "It's getting a little grungy."

"Sure," Elliott said, hopping on one foot, then the other.

"What color?"

"Black."

Mary snorted. "I don't think so."

"I like black," Elliott insisted, pulling Mary toward the door. "It's my favorite color. You can help me pick it out, but I gotta go. Pizza's coming."

"Okay, now listen. Seriously," Mary said, wearing her "Serious Mom" face. "I am NOT cleaning your room again until Christmas, at least. It can pile up to the ceiling for all I care. I'm not stepping foot in here. Got it?"

Elliott nodded and looked down the stairs at the front door.

Mary fought back a smile. "Okay, go."

CHAPTER 3

Elliott grabbed his baseball glove and ball to toss around while waiting for the pizza man. He hoped it wasn't a new driver. New drivers always had trouble finding their house, even though they were at the end of the cul-de-sac. After their house there was nowhere else to go but up a hill into the mass of forest and mountains.

As he walked down the driveway, he saw a car approaching. A lighted sign on top of the small automobile revealed it to be the pizza van. Elliott dug the wadded-up bills from his pocket and paid the driver. He then balanced the pizza box, his glove and his ball on top, as he trudged up the driveway.

The hot pizza smelled delicious. Elliott wanted to have a slice, but decided against it . . . after all, he didn't want to give the guys a reason not to let him join the game.

He cut across the driveway and walked through the front yard. He heard a loud crashing noise from the back of the house. Elliott froze.

"Harvey?" he called for his dog.

Harvey didn't come.

Elliott walked around the side of the house into the cluttered backyard and tried again. "Harvey? Is that you, boy?"

The haze from the forest had crept in, giving the outdoor furniture, the brittle stalks of corn from Mary's now-dying garden, and even the old toolshed a foggy, eerie quality. The glowing orange bug bulb that hung over the door of the toolshed made everything look even scarier.

The backyard was now quiet, except for the faint sounds of the radio playing from inside the house. Then a clanking sound came from the toolshed. Elliott placed the pizza box on wet, cold grass, never taking his eyes off the shed. He swallowed hard. Taking out the baseball, he tossed it into the open doorway of the shed.

"Fetch!" he said, hoping that Harvey would come running out. Instead, the ball was tossed back. It hit the ground and rolled to a stop in front of Elliott's sneaker-clad feet.

Harvey was nowhere in sight. Elliott was alone outside in the fog and the moonlight, and his eyes grew as large as saucers as they drank in the sight of the returned baseball.

"Mom!" he shrieked, turning and running for the safety of the house.

Obstacle number one: the pizza box.

Elliott tripped and stomped on the lid, his feet sliding out from under him as cardboard, hot cheese, and tomato sauce stuck together in a slippery mess. He fell backward in the grass, then scrambled to his feet, half running, half crawling for the back door of the house.

In the kitchen Michael and his friends continued their dungeon battles. He burst into the back door.

"Mom! Mom!" Elliott cried, pointing out at the backyard. "There's something out there!"

Michael snickered. "Ooh, big scary goblin

monster out to get the brave widdle elf?"

His mom looked at Elliott, his face as pale as frost. Something had frightened him.

"It's in the toolshed. It threw a ball at me."

"Sounds dangerous," Tyler wise-cracked, and the group went back to their game.

"I'm serious, guys!" Elliott yelled, grabbing their attention.

"Let's go look!" Michael said, pushing away from the table.

"No! Don't go out there!" Elliott protested, but no one was listening as the entire table of teenagers jumped up, ready for some real life adventure.

Mary raised a hand. "Stop. You guys stay right here."

"Don't worry, Mom, we'll check it out," Michael said.

"Safety in numbers," Steve agreed.

"Yeah!" Tyler added.

Tyler, Steve, and Michael marched out the door.

Greg hesitated, looking helplessly at Mary, not knowing if he should stay or go.

"I said, stay where you are," Mary commanded. Greg nodded.

Elliott tugged at Mary's arm. Mary sighed, pulled open a drawer, and took out a flashlight. She stepped outside, Elliott on her heels.

Greg stayed put, alone, until visions of being called a coward danced through his head. Taking a deep gulp of air, he finally followed, pausing long enough to grab a butcher knife out of the sink.

The army of boys, gathered tightly in a pack, crept across the backyard. Mary followed them with Elliott on her arm. Greg brought up the rear, waving his knife at unseen foes.

"What exactly did you see, Elliott?" she whispered.

"I don't know," Elliott replied, then pointed at the door of the toolshed. "But it's in there."

Mary pointed her flashlight at the shed entrance. Nothing unusual. Pots. Old boxes. Garden hose. Shovels.

"There's nothing in there," she said.

Michael leaned down, examining the concrete shed floor. "Look at these!" he said, pointing at several footprints left behind in a spilled bag of sand. While it was hard to tell exactly what kind of animal had made the tracks, it was obvious that they weren't human.

Michael stood up and crossed his arms. "The coyote's come back, Mom," he said.

Mary nodded in agreement. "Okay, party's over. Back in the house. Greg, give me that knife."

Greg placed the knife in Mary's hand as the group walked back.

"Oh, great! Nice job, Elliott!" Tyler said, holding up the crumpled pizza box. He opened the lid, which now was covered on the inside with a cheesy topping.

"It was an accident," Elliott said, embarrassed.

"You are such a geek," Tyler continued, tossing the box back to the ground.

"Mom, there *was* something. I swear," Elliott said.

"I know," Mary said tiredly. "There always is, honey."

The backyard grew silent once more . . .

Except, from deep within the toolshed behind a tipped-up wheelbarrow, where a most humanlike sigh of relief was exhaled.

Later that night Harvey's whimpering shook Elliott awake. The large yellow dog slept on the bottom bunk, while Elliott slept on the top.

A crashing sound of toppled trash cans came from the backyard.

Elliott's eyes raked the room. The clock on his desk said two A.M.

"Goblin time," he whispered to Harvey, tossing away the covers and dropping down to the floor. Dressed in layers for extra warmth, he crept down the hall, shooing Harvey back as he grabbed his jacket from the coatrack.

The flashlight his mother had used earlier was on the kitchen counter. Elliott thumbed the switch, and the bulb blazed into life. Following the beam, he walked into the backyard.

The pizza box was gone.

"Coyotes got it," he decided. Coyotes were the ones in the trash cans, too, he hoped.

Still, coyotes weren't known for being able to toss baseballs.

Elliott waved the beam over the tangled growth of Mary's dying vegetable garden, then stepped in among the tall cornstalks. The ground was churned up in places, and he saw more of the same footprints Michael had called "coyote tracks." He followed the trail, step by step.

Then the tracks stopped.

"Humph," Elliott muttered, pushing aside more of the stalks to reveal a strange face— one attached to a very wide head, with leathery skin, thin lips, and large, round eyes.

It was a face not of this world.

CHAPTER 4

Boy and alien gaped at each other in surprise, their faces glowing in the moonlight.

"Eeeee!" the creature screeched, turning and running away.

"Aaaaggghhh!" Elliott yelled, dropping his flashlight in shock.

The visitor smashed through the dried cornstalks and out the rear of the garden.

"Wait!" Elliott called, grabbing the flashlight and chasing the creature. "Don't go!"

The boy sprinted into the backyard and spied the small creature racing up the back of the hill to the rear gate. A streetlight by the metal gate illuminated the creature as he flipped up the latch and sped through, letting the metal door swing closed behind him.

Elliott ran up the stairs and looked out into the night. A grin broke out across his youthful face as he ran back down the stone steps. Thoughts of amazing creatures and mythical beings floated through his mind, only this was no card game at the kitchen table.

Early the next day Elliott had no interest in Saturday morning cartoons. He hopped on his bicycle, kicking up the kickstand as he rode down the driveway. He pedaled out of the cul-de-sac, and then out onto a dirt access road in the forest above his house.

Elliott parked the bike and took out a bag of multi-colored candies, tossing a few pieces here, a few pieces there, and calling out "Hello" and "I won't hurt you." He knew the creature must have entered the forest in this area, since it was a direct line down the hill to Elliott's backyard.

Elliott searched for the creature for over two hours, but the only living being he saw was a man, who appeared to be looking for something lost as well. The man's presence made Elliott nervous. He hid behind a tree and listened carefully.

A soft, jingling sound from a large ring of keys attached to his belt loop dogged the man's steps. Elliott waited until the man and the jingling sound had vanished, and then he began to lay a trail with the candies, creating a beeline back to his house.

The next move would be up to the creature.

Elliott hoped that, whatever it was, it liked candy.

At dinner that night Elliott slumped over his plate and picked at his baked potato.

Gertie, who was only five, shook her blond curls and tried to make conversation. She was still annoyed at having slept through the excitement the night before.

"What are you going as for Halloween, Elliott?" Gertie asked.

"I'm not going," Elliott said.

"Why don't you go as a goblin?" Michael suggested.

Elliott shot Michael an angry look.

"It's not that we don't believe you, honey," she began gently, but Elliott cut her off by hopping to his feet.

"It was real, I swear!"

"I'm going as a cowgirl," Gertie continued.

Elliott looked down at his little sister. "So? What else is new?" he demanded.

Michael took a bite of his Salisbury Steak. "Maybe it was an iguana," he said as he chewed.

"It was no iguana," Elliott said, annoyed.

"Or, you know how they say there are alligators in the sewers?" Michael continued, half seriously. "Could have been a gator."

Mary tried to place the train back on the proper track. "All I'm saying is that you probably just imagined it."

"I couldn't have imagined it," Elliott sighed.

Michael wasn't giving up so easily. He was now on a roll. "Maybe it was a pervert, or a deformed kid or something."

"It was nothing like that!" Elliott yelled.

Michael laughed, enjoying picking at his younger brother's sore spot. "I know!" he said in an Irish accent. "Maybe it was an elf or a leprechaun!"

"It was nothing like that, penis-breath!" Elliott yelled again.

"Elliott!" Mary commanded, trying to hide her smile. "Sit down."

Elliott sat and sulked. "Dad would believe me," he said sadly.

Mary used her napkin to wipe the corners of her mouth. "Why don't you call your father, then, and tell him about it?" she said, maintaining her composure.

"I can't," a resentful Elliott replied. "He's in Mexico. With Sally. Remember?"

Mary looked down at her plate. "If you see that thing outside again, whatever it is, don't go near it," she said tightly. "Call me and we'll have someone come and take it away."

"Like the dogcatcher?" Gertie asked.

"Exactly," Mary replied, pushing her chair away from the table.

Elliott plunged on, "But they'll give it a lobotomy or do experiments on it, or something!"

Mary stood, her "Stern Mom" mask starting to crack. "It's your turn to do the dishes, fellows."

"I set and cleared up," Michael said.

"*I* set and cleared up," Elliott whined in return.

Mary rubbed her temples.

"I did breakfast," Michael said.

"*I* did breakfast," Gertie insisted, joining the game.

Mary turned and walked out of the kitchen.

"What's the matter, Mom?" Michael asked, suddenly aware that all was not right.

"He hates Mexico," she said softly, leaving her plate on the counter as she stepped into the living room.

Michael reached over and smacked Elliott on the ear. "Way to go, man. Why don't you grow up? Don't talk about Sally in front of Mom. Think about how other people feel for a change."

Elliott stormed from the table, plate in hand. He almost hurled it into the sink, then turned on the hot water instead. Scraping the uneaten food into the garbage disposal, he glared out the window into the backyard, and the night.

CHAPTER 5

Hours later a waiting Elliott was curled up outside in his sleeping bag on a folding lawn chair. The lookout point was directly in front of the now brightly lit toolshed. Elliott had the area "staked out" for when the creature returned to the scene of the crime.

But his lookout plan wasn't working very well, because Elliott was sound asleep, snoring with his head on his arm. He held a dim flashlight in his right hand, which shined upward into the night sky.

Then a rustling sound came from the cornstalks. Elliott awoke in an instant to the sound of feet crunching through the garden. He held the position, watching as the creature once again approached the shed. He sat up and tried to call for his mother, but no sound came out of his throat.

The creature turned from the shed and slowly walked over to Elliott. Reaching out with one impossibly long-fingered hand, the being held it over Elliott's lap . . . and dropped a colorful handful of candy onto the sleeping bag.

Elliott smiled with relief, picked up one of the candies, and ate it. Then he gave another one back to the creature. The creature took the offering and munched on it, watching Elliott. Elliott rose from the chair and started leaving a new candy trail that led into the house. The creature followed, eating the candy as he walked through the kitchen, up the stairs, and into Elliott's room.

Elliott closed the door and took a deep breath. They had made it inside without waking anyone. The creature gazed at the posters on the walls and the clutter on the desk. He reached out to examine a box of pens and accidentally knocked it to the floor with a clatter.

Elliott winced, waiting to hear a knock at the door or the call of his mother, but nothing happened. He grabbed the blanket off his top bunk and tossed it over the visitor, just in case. After a minute, Elliott pulled back the blanket to reveal the alien's head.

The creature watched Elliott patiently. Elliott held a finger up to his lips and made a soft "shhh!" sound. The creature made the same motion, holding up a long finger to its own lips.

Elliott thought this was funny, so he held a finger to his ear, and the creature copied the action. Elliott held up his left hand with all five fingers spread apart. The visitor did the same, spreading his three fingers. Elliott held up one finger, and the creature did the same. They both wiggled their fingers.

Elliott was fascinated, but he was also very tired. He yawned and slowly walked backward, flopping down in a chair. The creature mimicked the motion, closing his eyes and finding a spot in the room to rest. They gazed wearily at each other and fell into a deep, peaceful sleep.

Back at the landing site, burrowed in the depths of the forest, men combed the area. The hour was late, but it allowed them to do their work undisturbed. Flash cameras popped, turning night into day as photographs were taken of the burn marks on the ground that the ship left when it took off.

A variety of hardware beeped and blinked as they examined the area. A jingle of keys could be heard as a man knelt down, running his fingers through the forest grass.

The man with the keys stood up, a tiny item held between thumb and forefinger.

It was a single yellow piece of candy.

On Monday morning, Mary stood on the rail of the lower bunk and held her hand to Elliott's forehead. Elliott rested on his back, looking up, his face droopy.

"Well," she said, "you do feel warm."

Elliott nodded as his mother shook the thermometer, then stuck it in his mouth.

"I'll be right back," she said, stepping out of the bedroom.

Elliott immediately took the thermometer out of his mouth and swung his gooseneck reading lamp over his head, holding it as closely to his face as he could. He also placed the thermometer against the lightbulb, for extra good measure.

Elliott heard the *clack clack clack* of his mother's high heels coming down the hallway, and he quickly swung the lamp back, sticking the thermometer in his mouth just in time.

Mary walked quickly into the bedroom. She took the thermometer from him and examined it as she approached the closet.

Elliott sat up as Mary swung the closet doors open and held his breath. Why was she going in the closet? he thought. Would she see the alien?

Mary turned, holding a quilt—a large, lumpy, alien-sized bundle of a quilt. Before Elliott could say a word, she shook out the bedding.

Luckily, nothing came tumbling out. Elliott flopped back down on the mattress with a sigh of relief as his mother tucked the quilt around his body.

She leaned in close to Elliott and gave him

a knowing look. "You waited outside for that thing to come back, didn't you?"

Elliott nodded.

"Can't keep spending nights outside. It's almost the end of October."

Elliott nodded again.

"Think you'll live if I go to work?"

Elliott nodded a third time.

"Okay, bye," Mary said, giving him a quick kiss on the cheek. "And no TV."

Then she was gone.

Elliott lay back on his pillow for a minute. For once, keeping a promise about watching television was NOT going to be a problem. He waited until he heard his mother's car pull away, then hopped down from his bunk and opened the closet door. The alien looked back at him. The creature was draped in Elliott's bathrobe.

"Good morning," Elliott said softly, gesturing for the being to step out of the closet. As the creature waddled out, Elliott asked, "Do you talk?"

No response.

"Me human. Boy. Elliott, Elliott, Elliott," Elliott said.

The creature pondered for a few seconds, then turned to walk over to Elliott's play table. The tabletop was covered with toys and debris. Elliott picked up objects and told him what they were.

"These are action figures. They can fight and have adventures. And this is a block. And that's money. A quarter."

Elliott pointed to the goldfish bowl. "That's a fish," he noted, dropping in a toy shark. "And that's a bigger fish. The bigger fish eat the little fish, but nobody eats the shark."

The creature reached over and picked up a toy car.

"That's a car. Car," Elliott said.

The creature promptly bit into the metal toy.

"No, no, no!" Elliott protested, pulling the car out of the alien's mouth. The creature peered back at Elliott, calmly blinking.

"Are you hungry?" Elliott asked as he padded over to the bedroom door and opened it. "I'm hungry. You stay here. Okay. Stay."

Elliott ran downstairs and into the kitchen. First he made two dripping peanut-butter-and-jelly sandwiches. Then he opened the refrigerator door again and grabbed an armload of more food, including the jar of peanut butter, milk, a loaf of bread, cheddar cheese, grape soda, an orange, an apple, and chocolate-chip cookie dough—only the best for his guest.

CHAPTER 6

That afternoon Michael was the first one home, and after football practice, he was quite annoyed to find there was nothing left to eat in the refrigerator but vegetables and ice water. There could only be one explanation for the lack of food, and it was currently upstairs playing sick.

Mike ran into Elliott's room. "How you feeling, faker?" he said. "See you cleaned out the fridge."

"What time is it?" Elliott asked, standing in the middle of his room in his pajamas.

"After five. Mom'll be here soon. Hey, Tyler said he got sixty-nine thousand at Asteroid yesterday, but he pulled the plug, so, who knows—"

Elliott held up a hand for quiet. "I've got something really important to tell you."

"Okay. What?"

"This is the most important, probably the most serious thing ever."

Michael's eyes narrowed. "What'd you do?"

"Nothing!" Elliott said. "Remember the goblin?"

Michael shot Elliott a look of disbelief, as he spied a quart of milk on Elliott's table. "You're so lame, Elliott."

Elliott got down from the bed and tugged on Michael's football jersey. "He came back," Elliott whispered.

Michael sniffed the milk, then took a long drink from the carton. "Bull," he said.

"Come on," Elliott said, "I'll show you."

Michael followed his younger brother across the room to the closet door.

"One thing. I have absolute power. Say it."

Michael was losing his patience. "What have you got in here? Is it the coyote? Let me see it!"

"No. Swear first. The most excellent promise you can make."

Michael groaned. "Okay, okay. He's all yours. Mom's going to kill you."

Elliott pointed to the wall opposite the door. "Stand over there. And you'd better take off your shoulder pads."

"What?"

"You might scare him. Go on."

Michael removed his shoulder pads as Elliott opened up the closet, stepped inside, and pulled the doors shut.

"And close your eyes."

"Don't push it."

"I'm not coming out until your eyes are closed."

Michael squeezed his eyes shut. "They're closed, okay? Happy?"

Elliott and the creature stepped out of the closet. Elliott gave the little alien a quick grin, put an arm over his shoulders, and nodded reassuringly.

"Swear it, Michael. One more time. I have ab—"

"You have absolute power," Michael groaned. "All right, already!"

At that instant Gertie chose to burst into the room, her rag doll in tow.

"Elliott! Elliott!" she called and then was struck dumb. She looked at the creature who peered back, his neck extending to scope out the little girl.

Michael opened his eyes and looked at the goggle-eyed Gertie.

Elliott opened his mouth to speak.

Too late.

"EEEEEEK!" Gertie screamed, pointing and hopping up and down.

The creature shrieked back, giving as good as he got.

Michael also screamed, staggering backward into the wall and succeeding in pulling down a bookshelf onto his head.

Even Elliott screamed, more in frustration than fright, but he caught himself. "Make her stop!" he hissed, pointing at Gertie.

Michael stood there, his mouth opening and closing like a fish out of water.

"Michael!" Elliott yelled.

Michael snapped out of the shock and clamped a hand over Gertie's mouth.

"In the closet! Fast!" Elliott barked. Michael obeyed, pulling their sister into the closet Elliott and Gertie shared. Elliott pushed the creature in too, a pile of stuffed animals falling on them as he slammed the door with a bang.

Just as the closet door closed, Mary walked into the room. "Hi, honey . . . what happened in here?" she asked, looking at the fallen shelving, the piles of toys and books on the floor, the mountains of clothing. "I just cleaned this room three days ago!"

Elliott draped himself over the arm of a stuffed chair and tried to stay calm. "What do you mean?" he replied, innocently.

Mary lifted her arms and waved them about over his desk. "I mean, this! Look at this! How is this possible?"

Elliott stood up, stepping as far away from the closet door as possible, and dropped the innocent act in case his mom got suspicious. "Ohhhh. You mean my room."

"This isn't a room," Mary said, reaching down and picking up a half-eaten bowl of cereal. "This is an accident."

Elliott stared at the floor. "I'll clean it," he said.

Mary sat the bowl of cereal down on the dresser and stepped over to kiss Elliott on the forehead. "This must mean that you're feeling well enough to go to school tomorrow . . . although, you do seem to be sweating."

Elliott nodded.

"Okay, clean," Mary said, pointing at the largest pile of dirty laundry. "And keep an eye on Gertie while I take a shower."

"For sure," Elliott answered as his mother finally left the room.

"Don't forget to vacuum," she called as she went into her own bedroom.

Elliott willed himself to stand still and count to ten, and then he dashed across the debris to the closet door. He stepped inside, standing beside his sister and brother. All three of them stood quietly, Gertie extra silent since Michael still had a hand over her mouth.

They peered at the fourth member of their quartet in the crowded closet. A single naked bulb dangled from the ceiling, creating shadows that flickered on the walls. Elliott took a deep breath. He looked at Michael, then Gertie, then down at the alien, who blinked up at him.

"I'm keeping him," Elliott whispered.

CHAPTER 7

"You gotta tell Mom," Michael said.

"She'll want to do the right thing. You know what that means, don't you?" Elliott pointed to the creature. "Dog food. Or lobotomy."

"What *is* it?" Michael wondered, squatting for a better look. The creature obliged, eye-balling Michael with equal interest.

"He's good. I can feel it," Elliott said.

Michael drummed his fingers on Gertie's cheek. "She'll blab it for sure."

"Nuh-uh!" Gertie protested from behind Michael's palm, then squealed with uncertainty as the creature trained his large eyes on her.

"Gertie, he's not going to hurt you," Elliott

said, smiling reassuringly at his sister. "Honest."

Gertie thought this over, then gave a nod.

Michael loosened his grip, anticipating screams and cries for mommy.

But Gertie just looked the creature up and down. "Is he a boy or a girl?" she asked.

"Ah . . . he's a boy," Elliott said.

"How do you know?" Gertie said with a shrug.

Elliott ignored the question. "Now, you're not going to tell, are you? You can't even tell Mom."

"Why not?"

"Because, um," Elliott paused, searching for the right phrase. "Because grown-ups can't see him. Only kids can see him."

Gertie looked doubtful. "Give me a break," she said.

Elliott glanced at Michael. His older brother frowned and nodded. They needed to do something more drastic to convince her.

"Do it, Mike. We have to," Elliott ordered.

Michael grabbed away the floppy rag doll that Gertie had been carrying.

"Hey!" Gertie cried.

Michael wrenched the doll's arm behind its back.

"No! No! Please don't break my arm!" Michael said in a high-pitched voice, speaking for the doll. "Please! I'll do anything! Help me, Gertie!"

Gertie's eyes filled with tears.

The creature craned his neck, observing all of this, his own large dark eyes mirroring Gertie's pain.

"Stop it! Stop it!" Gertie squealed, trying to pull the doll away from Michael.

"Promise not to tell," Elliott said, holding firm.

Gertie sniffed, holding back her tears. "Yes. I promise."

"For sure?"

Gertie nodded.

"That goes for you, too, Mike," Elliott said.

Michael returned the doll to Gertie. "No problem, bro."

"Is he from the moon?" Gertie asked, looking at the back of the alien's head.

"Maybe," Elliott said. "Yeah, sure. The moon. Isn't that exciting?"

Gertie eyeballed the creature. "He's funny-looking," she decided.

"Was he wearing any clothes?" Michael asked.

"Nope. Not a stitch."

"Kids! Come help with dinner! Everybody!" Mary called from downstairs.

"Okay, then," Elliott said. "Act normal."

The kids filed out of the closet, leaving the creature hiding inside.

"Stay," Elliott whispered, peeking through the slats of the closet door. The creature peered back peacefully, silent among the clothing and the toys.

After scarfing down the simple meal of burgers and chips, Elliott wiped his mouth with a paper napkin. "Delicious!" he said, picking up his plate and crossing to the kitchen sink.

Michael rose and added his plate to Elliott's.

"Mama?" said Gertie.

"Yes, sweetie?" Mary said.

"Why do I see what you don't see?"

Elliott and Michael froze.

"Because we're different people, we see things differently," Mary replied.

"What about the people who aren't people?" a confused Gertie asked.

"May I take your plate?" Elliott interrupted, reaching for the remains of Mary's hamburger dinner.

Mary chuckled, amused at Elliott's sudden burst of manners. "Why, thank you, kind sir."

"There's no such thing, Gertie, as people who aren't people," Michael said.

Mary stood and stretched. "I've got stuff to do. Will you finish up in here?"

"Absolutely," Elliott said with a wide smile.

Michael and Gertie also grinned.

Mary's "Mom Sense" tingled, but only for a brief second. Whatever was afoot could wait.

After Mary left the dining room, Elliott began to pile leftovers onto a plate for their guest. "Michael, watch Mom. When the coast is clear, you can come in. Knock three times."

"The coast is clear right now," Michael said. "I'm going with you."

They both looked at their sister.

"Stay put," Elliott said.

"Yeah," Michael added.

Gertie gave them her best wide-eyed innocent look. Of course, her brothers didn't buy it for a minute.

They exited and Gertie waited patiently until Mary returned.

"What are you doing, Gertie?" Mary asked, glancing up from a laundry basket of towels she was getting ready to fold.

"I'm going to play in Elliott's room," Gertie replied.

"Okay," Mary said, returning to her towels. "Don't let them torture you."

Gertie continued past Mary's open door to the head of the stairs. A droopy geranium, almost dead, sat in a pretty red pot in a corner, far away from sunlight. Gertie picked up the plant and carried it to Elliott's door. She'd seen her mom take a plant when visiting company on more than one occasion, and even though she was only five, she was already a firm believer in good manners.

She knocked at the door three times. Michael let her in.

"What's with the flower?" he asked.

Gertie pointed at the creature. "It's for him," she said.

"Be careful he doesn't eat it," Michael muttered.

The creature perked up at the sight of the plant, watching intently as Gertie sat it on the table next to the now-empty plate that Elliott had brought in earlier.

Backing away from their visitor, the kids spoke in whispers.

"Maybe he's just some animal that wasn't supposed to live," Michael theorized. "You know, like those sick baby rabbits we saw that time."

Elliott gave a dismissive wave. "Don't be a doofus," he said.

The creature did not respond. He had focused his attention on the various balls of clay that littered Elliott's tabletop. He stared at the clay for a moment, then waddled over to the window, looking at the night sky.

"I got an idea," Elliott said. "Get the atlas."

Michael pulled a red-covered atlas from one of the bookshelves. He laid it on the tabletop and began to leaf through the contents.

"What are we doing?"

Elliott stuck out a hand to stop Michael from turning pages. The atlas was now open to a double-page spread of the United States.

The creature turned and watched the humans, fascinated as always at their movements, their speech, their emotions.

Elliott pointed at the pages. "Look. See? This is where we are."

Michael brought down a globe from the shelf. "Here, use this," he suggested.

Elliott closed the book and pointed at the North American continent on the globe. "See?" he said to the creature. "We're here. Where are you from?"

The creature looked at the globe, then at Elliott, then turned and pointed.

His long narrow finger was pointed at the night sky and the yellow crescent moon, both now visible through the window.

"I don't like his feet," Gertie decided.

"Shh! He's trying to tell us something."

Elliott opened the atlas again, flipping pages until he found a drawing of the solar system. The creature reached out and laid a hand on the page.

"Earth," Elliott said, rubbing a finger under the picture in the atlas, and then gesturing toward the globe. "Yeah, Earth. Home."

Then one by one the five clay balls on Elliott's desk rose up from the tabletop and orbited above them.

The creature pointed to the map, then to the hovering balls. He pointed to the globe and to Elliott . . . then to one small ball and himself.

Elliott felt a chill race up his spine. "Oh, no," he whispered.

"Elliott, what does it mean?" Michael asked in a shaky voice.

Before Elliott could answer, the creature jerked his large head toward the window, as if startled by a noise. In the same moment all of the clay balls fell to the floor.

Elliott shivered, his face a mirror of the creature's worried expression.

Michael looked at Elliott, then at the creature. He walked over and tried to peer through the window into the darkness.

"What is it?" he asked.

"I don't know," Elliott said. "Something scary."

Gertie pulled at the hem of Elliott's shirt. "What's scary?" she demanded.

Elliott whirled and shouted at his sister. "I

don't know!" he snapped. "I don't know, okay?"

The creature extended his long arms, as if trying to herd the children forward, pushing them toward the open door of the closet. The kids obliged, their faces curious, but confused.

Elliott broke away. "You stay put. All of you," he said. "Michael, watch him. And Gertie."

Michael didn't argue. He pulled Gertie close and closed the door, securing the three of them in the closet.

Elliott went into the hallway, creeping past his mother's bedroom and down the stairs. The boy wasn't sure what he was looking for, but he knew it was outside, so he exited the front door.

Nothing. Not even the sound of insects. He held his breath.

Then there was a sound, a faint, jingling noise, like sleigh bells . . . or a ring of keys.

Elliott flattened against the wall of the house and inched his way into the backyard. He peeked around the corner and found only a quiet, empty backyard. Feeling slightly foolish, Elliott stepped out into the middle of the yard and put his hands on his hips.

Another jingle could be heard, followed by a series of clicking sounds, and this time the sounds came from atop the hill that adjoined the property. Elliott didn't hesitate, but strode toward the noises, walking heavily up the brick steps to the backyard gate.

The wire-mesh gate was open, swinging gently on its rusty hinges. Elliott shivered in the cool night air, then slammed the gate shut. The clicking sound had stopped. The jingle of the keys was gone.

The only sound now was the beating of his heart, pounding hard in his ears.

CHAPTER 8

Later that night, after everyone went to sleep, the creature sat comfortably inside the closet, Elliott's bathrobe draped around his shoulders like a woolen cape. He was too excited to sleep.

Instead, he waited and watched, peering through the slats of the door at the sleeping Elliott. The creature looked around the room, his gaze falling on Gertie's drooping geranium.

Suddenly the flower pivoted on its stem, turning to face the closet and the visitor inside. As it moved, the geranium began to straighten, and in a burst of life, the tight buds bloomed into vibrant red and yellow flowers.

Within the closet the creature nodded, pleased, and returned to a stack of Gertie's books. He had been leafing through a book called *My ABC's*. It lay open on the floor as the creature carefully turned the pages with his long, skinny fingers.

He stopped on the letter *B*. An illustration of a boy was next to the letter. The creature strummed his fingers on the drawing of the boy.

"Ell-ee-ott," he said in a soft, reedy voice, like the voice of an old man discovering language for the very first time. "Ell-ee-ott."

The next morning Mary raced about gearing up for another day at work. Then she charged out of the house with Gertie in tow to take her to school.

Elliott and Michael left the house and walked toward their bus stop. Neither of them spoke. They were worried, although for different reasons.

After a few silent minutes Michael decided to say something. "Okay, so, like, he hears real good and can move stuff without touching it, and he—oh, God, Elliott! How do you know there aren't more of them?"

Elliott wasn't concerned. "There aren't," he said flatly. "He's alone."

"How do you know?" Michael demanded.

Elliott stopped walking, scanning a uniformed man across the street. "I just know, okay? He's alone. Any moron can see that."

"Says you."

"Is that our regular milkman?"

Michael looked. "Sure. So, who was creeping around outside the house last night?"

"I think he was looking for . . ."—Elliott struggled for the right word—*"him."*

"You gotta tell, Elliott. It's too serious."

"No!" Elliott cried, stopping in his tracks. "I have absolute power. You said so! He needs time, Michael. He wants to stay with us. He has to plan his strategy."

Michael frowned at his brother as if Elliott were the alien. "How do you know what he wants? Is he in your brain or something?"

"Or something."

Michael began waving his arms and yelling in Elliott's face. "Aw, come on. He's a man from outer space, Elliott! A real life extra-terrestrial! We could all wake up and find our-selves on Mars or something, surrounded by millions of these little squashy guys."

"Don't get crazy," Elliott said as they turned a corner and headed for the gathering of kids waiting at the bus stop.

"This is an excellent time to get crazy!" Michael retorted. "And besides, maybe he's not smart enough to plan any strategy. Maybe he's like a worker bee who only knows how to push buttons or something."

"He is smart!" an offended Elliott replied. "And he's . . . good. It's weird. It's like I know how he feels. And he's good, I can tell."

"Well, you'd better think nice-nice about him," Michael said, unconvinced. "Just in case he decides you're the enemy."

"Hey, Elliott! Where's your goblin?" Tyler's voice cried out. He stepped forward, snicker-ing and pointing at Elliott.

"Shut up," Michael said.

"Did he come back?" Steve asked.

Elliott ignored the older boys, turning away to face Greg.

"So, did he?" Greg demanded.

"Yeah, he came back," an angry Elliott replied. "He came back and he wasn't a goblin. He was a spaceman!"

Michael slugged Elliott on the arm. "Quiet, Elliott," he muttered.

The other boys cracked up.

"Oh, radical, man," Tyler said, trying to control his laughter.

This is going to be the longest day of my life, Elliott thought to himself as he watched the bus pull up to the curb.

The creature waddled into the kitchen, Elliott's robe over his shoulders, looking like a little old man in search of his morning cup of coffee. Harvey followed him closely. Obviously, the alien smelled like nothing of this Earth, and it was driving Harvey's nose into a fit.

He was alone. No voices. No Ell-ee-ott.

The refrigerator started to hum. The creature cocked his head, listening, his mouth open as he focused on the sound.

He reached out with a fingertip and touched the door. No response.

He gripped the handle of the icebox door and pulled. The door swung open, revealing a chilly interior. The creature's face wrinkled as the aromas wafted out. Harvey took notice as well, and began to whimper and beg. An open refrigerator door meant only one thing: a possible treat for Harvey.

The creature reached in and selected the first container, pulling back the lid to reveal a pale yellow substance—old, uneaten, should-have-been-thrown-out-days-ago potato salad.

The alien scooped out a sample and tasted it. If his wizened face could have wrinkled more, it would have. The creature continued to sort through the contents, opening, tasting, and discarding items on the kitchen floor—much to Harvey's delight.

Then he came upon a cluster of metallic canisters. Intrigued, the creature brought out the six cans, all attached at the tops by a plastic ring. He pulled one free and managed to open the pop-top. The can opened with a *Pssst!* under one pull from the alien's long, skinny finger.

He sniffed the liquid inside. Pungent, yet

appealing. And he was very, *very* thirsty. Without a second thought the alien tipped back the cold can of beer and poured all twelve ounces down his throat.

CHAPTER 9

Today was a special day in biology class, but Elliott could have cared less. He was busy sketching pictures of the creature in his lab notebook. He was an alien, an extra-terrestrial, an "E.T." Elliott thought, and grinned. *E.T.* He wrote the name over the sketch.

At the front of the lab, the teacher droned on. "So we're going to peel the skin back and take a look inside the frog. You'll notice that the lungs will not collapse—"

Elliott burped. Unfortunately, this was no small belch, but a loud "Bracccck!" His classmates giggled. The teacher continued.

"The heart will go on beating for a short time after the death of the frog. You'll get to see it yourself if you work quickly."

Elliott looked at his frog. The green and brown creature tried to climb up the sides of the glass jar, but kept falling down, trapped, a prisoner.

Back home the alien wandered into the family playroom, a can of beer in each hand. Harvey trailed along, hoping for more treats from his new best friend. Popping open another can, the creature knocked back the brew in a single long gulp. Suddenly he didn't feel so good. His eyes were glassy and heavy, and his stomach felt like it wanted to crawl out of his mouth.

Gertie's Speak & Spell toy was on the sofa. The creature craned his head down for a closer look. The simple array of controls seemed straightforward enough, even if the letters were still unfamiliar.

Extending a finger from his free hand, the alien pressed a button.

"C," the toy said. "Can you spell 'cat'?"

The alien could not. Another gadget now

had his attention. The television remote control was on the sofa next to the Speak & Spell. He ran a finger down the buttons of the remote and the television sprang to life.

The creature watched a cartoon cat scramble after a cartoon mouse, then pressed another button on the remote.

Click.

A human woman danced with a mop across a gleaming kitchen floor.

Click.

An older human, a man, sat behind a desk and talked and talked.

Click. Click. Click.

So many images, all fascinating. Despite feeling queasy, the alien decided to have another beer to celebrate his latest discovery. Oddly enough, the pop-top did not open as easily as it had the previous five times, but the creature kept to it, and he was soon guzzling the last of the six pack.

The alien slumped against the sofa, now flipping channels easily like a human. Harvey idly licked the last of the potato salad off the dangling fingers of the creature's free hand. Sitting up, the alien tried to peer at the dog, but he couldn't keep his head from wobbling.

"Bracccck!" the creature burped, as he continued to mindlessly absorb the images on the screen.

"All right, I'm going to place a cotton ball soaked with ether in each jar, and while we wait for the frogs to expire, we will ready our tools."

Elliott grinned at his lab partner, a cute little blond girl whose name he couldn't remember to save his life, or even his frog's life, for that matter. But suddenly Elliott felt quite sad. He leaned in close to his jar, his face smack up against the side, and he gazed at his doomed frog.

The frog looked back, no longer struggling to climb free. There was a look of defeat in his sad brown eyes.

Elliott drew himself up and in a cracking voice asked his teacher: "Are you just going to let the poor, defenseless thing die?"

The teacher didn't respond as he dropped

A mysterious spaceship lands in the forest. . . .

The search party is on the lookout.

What's that noise in the toolshed?

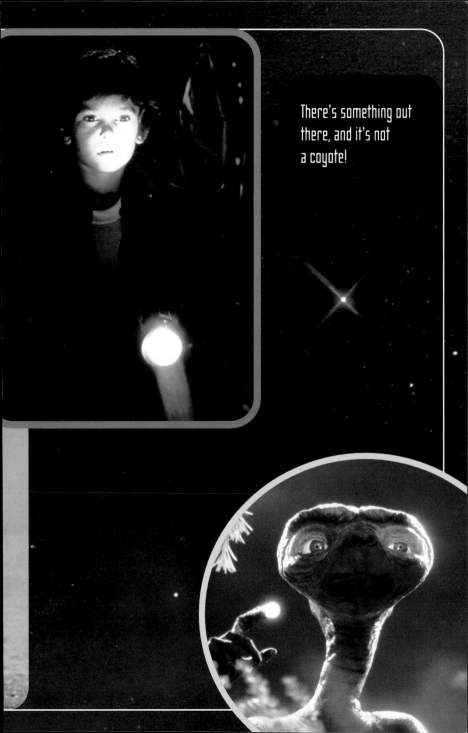

There's something out there, and it's not a coyote!

Let's play in Elliott's room!

Gertie isn't the only one who likes to dress up.

E.T. phone home?

"Tell me when it's over!"

Don't worry, Elliott. E.T.'s going to be okay.

Off to the forest!

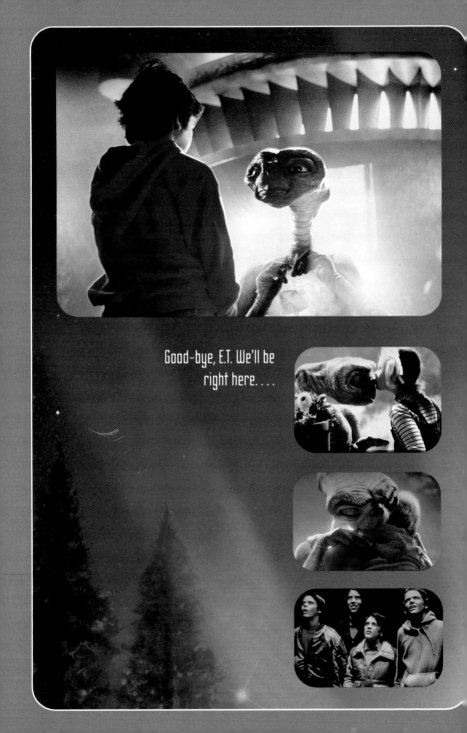

Good-bye, E.T. We'll be
right here....

an ether-soaked cotton ball into Elliott's jar and closed the lid.

The creature had given up for the moment on television and was now gazing at the morning newspaper Mary had left behind on the kitchen table. He was reading the funnies and one of the comic strips got his full drunken attention.

The daily episode came from *Flash Gordon*. In the strip Flash had crashed his ship and was now carrying an emergency distress beacon to a hilltop. In the last panel the machine came to life, sending radar waves out into space as part of a futuristic call for help.

The alien lifted his head from the newspaper. Even in his tipsy mode, he knew what he must do. From the playroom the sounds of the television floated across the kitchen. A commercial was playing for the phone company, which asked viewers to "reach out and touch someone."

Back in the classroom laboratory, Elliott snapped to attention.

He gazed at his dying frog with a determined grimace. "Reach out. Save him," he whispered. "Got to reach out and save him."

Elliott picked up the jar. His blond lab partner looked at him with a mix of disdain and confusion. Elliott had always been a little weird, she thought, but today he was entering new realms of strangeness.

Inside the jar the frog gave a weak dying kick. Elliott unscrewed the lid and dumped the frog to the floor. The frog hopped under the lab table as Elliott ran to the next station and snatched another jar, shaking loose a second frog.

"Elliott! Stop that!" the teacher cried, but Elliott wasn't listening. All he could hear was the voice of freedom, and the desire to be saved.

"Run for your lives!" Elliott shrieked, running and freeing more frogs. "Back to the river! Back to the forest!"

The other students were now getting into the spirit, letting their own frogs loose from the jars. A large aquarium filled with frogs was flipped over, freeing dozens of croaking, hopping frogs which fell onto the floor. The teacher scrambled, trying to gather them up. Elliott, laughing with delight, grabbed up a handful and dropped them out of the window to the waiting bushes.

Back home the creature laughed as well . . . a musical sound. He was back on the sofa, now flipping channels at will. *Click.* Another cartoon. *Click.* A love story. A man gave a woman a passionate kiss.

Back at school Elliott reached up to his lab partner, pulled her head back, and gave her a big kiss on the lips.

Inside the playroom the creature reached down woozily and held Harvey's head, giving the confused dog a kiss before tumbling off the sofa and landing on his back on the rug.

CHAPTER 10

When the creature woke up from his drunken stupor, he staggered to his feet and took another look at the *Flash Gordon* comic strip.

Cooing with excitement, he began to gather items from the shelves and tables of the house, placing them with care on a blanket on the floor.

First, the blender, followed by the knobs off the stove. A pincushion stuffed with pins. The kitchen radio off the windowsill. Tinfoil-wrapped leftovers from within the refrigerator. An empty coffee can. A pair of toy walkie-talkies. An electric pencil sharpener.

At school the children were running around the classroom, tripping, trying to catch and release more frogs to the wild.

"Come with me, young man," the angry science teacher hissed, grabbing Elliott by a bicep and marching the boy toward the door.

Helpless, his mind now racing with ways to free himself from his teacher's iron grip, Elliott struggled as he was escorted down the hallway to the principal's office.

At home the creature sighed. He needed that other item, the colorful machine that spoke in the language of children.

So the Speak & Spell joined the rest of the hardware, which he now pulled in a jumbled heap in front of the television. On the screen puppets were singing and dancing.

The alien used a screwdriver he'd found in Mary's kitchen tool drawer and flipped off the back plate of the toy, revealing the wiring. He touched a computer chip with a fingertip. Harvey's ears popped up and he barked a warning, but the creature paid no mind, his attention fully on the Speak & Spell.

The back door opened, and Mary walked to the far side of the kitchen, her view of the mess on the floor hidden by the cabinets. She dropped a bag of groceries on the counter, then flipped through the handful of mail she'd retrieved from the bottom of the driveway.

Back in the nurse's office at school, the tiny waiting room was empty, yet the posters on the walls, the tile floor, and even parts of the wooden furniture were covered in a childish scrawl. A closer look revealed the wiring pattern inside the Speak & Spell.

A path could be traced from the waiting room into the examining room where Elliott was writing. The white walls, the white sink, the white medicine chest, and even the white linoleum floor were covered in black marker patterns.

Meanwhile, Gertie, wearing her full cowgirl ensemble from school, ran into the kitchen, past the mess on the floor, and into the playroom. The creature didn't even glance up.

"Here he is!" Gertie said happily.

"Here who is?" Mary asked idly, frowning at the bill she held in her hands.

"The man from the moon."

"Oh!" Mary laughed. "Well, that *is* a wonderful surprise."

Gertie smiled down at the alien. The creature looked up and smiled back.

"What are you doing down here?" Gertie asked. "You're supposed to be upstairs!"

The alien returned to his labors, pulling apart the electric pencil sharpener.

"Look at how much work you've done! Were you scared being here all by yourself? Was Harvey nice to you?"

The phone rang.

"Hello?" Mary answered, picking up the receiver, then stepping into the hallway away from the kitchen. "Yes, this is she. What? Wait, how do you mean 'acting strangely'?"

The television began showing an episode of *Sesame Street*. Big Bird greeted the viewers with a wave and a smile. "Hi, kids!" Big Bird said.

Harry Monster shoved his way into the picture. "Hello, monsters," he added.

"And hello to the monsters," Big Bird agreed.

Mary spoke softly into the phone receiver, striving to maintain her composure. "Well, he was feeling ill yesterday, but . . . intoxicated?" she said in disbelief. "Are you sure you have the right Elliott?"

The alien paid the TV screen no mind. The

innards of the walkie-talkies were proving much more intriguing than pretend puppet monsters. But Gertie sat glued to the set, paying her own real life "monster" no mind as she watched the Muppets present the letter of the day.

"Today's show is brought to you by the letter *B*," Big Bird said cheerily.

"Beeeeee," Gertie said, looking at the creature. "Bee. Bee. B. B. B."

The alien worked on. Gertie plopped her cowgirl hat on the top of his wide head. The creature paused to turn and gaze at the human child sitting next to him.

Gertie "beeped" him on the nose. "B. B. B."

The creature looked at her patiently. "Beeeeee," he said obligingly.

Gertie's mouth fell open as she clapped her hands with delight. "B! You said B! Good!"

"B. Good," the creature said. Gertie stared at him wide-eyed.

"Gertie, where are you, honey?" Mary called as she hung up the telephone.

Gertie stood up on the sofa and waved, jumping up and down so she could see her mother. The creature, seated on the floor behind the television set, was hidden from Mary's view from the kitchen.

"Here I am!"

"Gertie, I have to go pick up Elliott at school. Can you be a good girl and stay here and watch *Sesame Street*? I'll be back in ten minutes."

Gertie pointed at the hidden creature. "Mama, I know you can't see him, but he can talk!" she said proudly.

"Of course he can talk," Mary said absently, searching for her car keys in her purse. "Now, you stay there."

Mary ran out of the back door. Gertie shrugged, then slid back down to the floor and gave the creature a big smile.

"Hi!" she chirped with a wave.

"Hi," the alien replied, waving his own long hand. He paused, then pointed at the telephone on the coffee table.

"That's a phone," Gertie told him. "Phone."

"Fuh-on," the creature repeated.

"You want to call somebody?" Gertie asked.

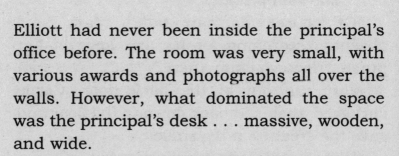

CHAPTER 11

Elliott had never been inside the principal's office before. The room was very small, with various awards and photographs all over the walls. However, what dominated the space was the principal's desk . . . massive, wooden, and wide.

The boy sat on one side and peered across the expanse at the principal, who was examining Elliott with equal intensity.

"So," the principal said. "Tell me what it is, son. Pot? Quaaludes?"

Elliott looked back in sheer hopelessness. He had no idea what to say.

At home Gertie had dressed the alien in her cowgirl hat and belt. The creature had gathered up the various disassembled items into a pile on the blanket. Completing his work would take time. He needed to finish it upstairs, where it was safer and quieter.

The cowboy creature stood at the foot of the stairs, the blanket of items he had harvested wrapped into a large, lumpy bundle.

A bundle too heavy for a stubby alien and a little girl to pull up the stairs.

The creature gave the equivalent of a human sigh, stared at the bundle, and concentrated. Watching this, Gertie concentrated on the bundle too, staring at the blanket of goodies with her most ferocious scowl.

As if in reply, the bundle moved.

Gertie giggled. The creature focused harder. *Bump.* The bundle lumbered up onto the first step. *Bump. Bump.* The second and third step . . .

"One. Two. Three . . . ooops!" Gertie said, counting along until the bundle fell backward, landing in a heap at the bottom of the stairs.

The creature blinked, suddenly appearing very weak and frail, but only for a few seconds.

Then he opened his eyes and began to concentrate once more.

Bump. Bump. Bump.

As the principal continued to drone on, Elliott felt the chair beneath him move. More of a hop, really. The chair rose a foot in the air, then fell.

Bump.

The principal, his glasses off as he swiped at the lenses, heard the sound and gave a slight grin. "Nice to know you're still alive over there. I mean, I see you fine young people searching for an escape at such a tender age. I know there are lots of temptations out there."

Elliott and his chair rose into the air, hanging in space, levitating in place. His head almost touched the ceiling.

"Sure, the world looks like a hopeless, cruel place," the principal said, still looking down at his glasses as he cleaned them with his tie. "But resorting to drugs and liquor is no answer."

The speech over, he placed his glasses back on his face and looked at Elliott, or rather, at Elliott's sneakered feet. The man blinked as the sight of the levitating boy and chair finally registered.

"Uh," the principal said, before the chair crashed back to the floor, a mere second before Mary opened the door.

"Mom!" Elliott said, but before anyone else could speak, the principal held up a hand for quiet. Mary peered at the older man, a bit concerned. He looked quite pale and queasy, as if he were about to collapse, or at least throw up on his wide, expansive desktop.

But the principal did neither. He stood up and smoothed his shirt. "Yes, ah, this is your mother? That's a fine idea, coming by, yes. A little rest is we . . . I mean, all *you* need. I'm sure this was all some sort of misunderstanding."

Elliott stood and Mary placed a possessive hand on his shoulder. "Can I go now, sir?" the boy asked.

"Yes," the principal said. "Please. Dismissed."

Mary's mouth opened and closed as she

tried to understand why the principal was acting so strangely, but before she could say anything, Elliott took her hand and led her from the room. "We'll talk in the car, Mom."

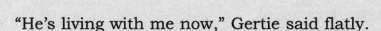

CHAPTER 12

"He's living with me now," Gertie said flatly.

Elliott snorted, pushing past his younger sister and heading for the closet door of her bedroom . . . the same closet that adjoined his room.

The creature stood erect as Elliott stepped inside. The closet was now more of a "nesting area" than ever before, and was littered with the scavenged household appliances and objects. However, it wasn't the disassembled appliances and toys that had Elliott's eye, but what Gertie had done to the creature.

He was now a she, dressed up in one of Mary's old curly wigs, a veiled hat, a fox stole, and lots of costume jewelry.

"Elliott," the creature said.

Elliott's face broke out in a wide, goofy grin.

"I taught him to talk," Gertie said proudly. "He can talk now."

Elliott stepped closer and removed the woman's hat from the creature's wide head, nearly stepping on the mess of wires and components from the guts of the Speak & Spell toy.

"You talked to me," Elliott breathed, his mind thinking of what he had been drawing in class earlier. An alien. A visitor. An extra-terrestrial.

"E.T." Elliott announced. "Can you say that? I'm Elliott and you're E.T."

"E.T.," the creature agreed.

Elliott removed the dress-up items and shoved them at his sister. "You should give him back his dignity."

Gertie shot Elliott a dirty look as he pushed her out of the closet. Behind him, E.T. took a deep breath, then spoke:

"Phone."

Elliott turned and kneeled down to look at E.T. "Phone?" he asked.

E.T. picked up the newspaper and pointed to the Flash Gordon cartoon. He handed the

sheet to Elliott, then walked into Elliott's bedroom and pointed at the window.

"Home," the creature said.

Elliott nodded. "E.T. home."

"E.T. home. Phone."

Understanding dawned on Elliott. "E.T.
phone home?"

"E.T. phone home."

"And . . . they'll come?"

E.T. lowered his head. "Come."

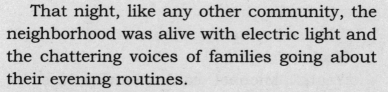

That night, like any other community, the
neighborhood was alive with electric light and
the chattering voices of families going about
their evening routines.

Down the street a white van crept, listening, seeking . . . tracking.

Then Michael's voice sounded from the
garage: "I guess we should just get anything
that looks like he could use it for his machine."

The van stopped. A man sat inside behind a
bank of high-tech surveillance gear, listening.

"What would make radar?" Elliott asked.

"How do I know? You're the genius here.

You have absolute power. 'I found him. He belongs to me.' Remember?" Michael said angrily, blowing the dust off a soldering iron and tossing it into a cardboard box already filled with tools, fuses, wires, and anything else to be found in the cabinets and workbenches of the garage.

Elliott sensed his brother's frustration. "What's wrong?"

"It's just . . . this place. The garage," Michael said. "We haven't really hung out here since Dad left."

"Oh," Elliott agreed, sitting down on a stool next to his brother.

"We used to have fun out here, didn't we?"

"Yeah."

"Yeah," Michael said wistfully, lost in thought. He picked up a radial saw blade and added it to the cardboard box. "You know, Elliott . . . the creature. He's not looking so good lately."

"Don't say that!" Elliott protested. "We're fine!"

"What's this 'we' stuff? You say 'we' all the time now," Michael said, picking up the box and moving to the other side of the garage.

"And I'm not kidding. I think he might be getting sick."

"He's fine," Elliott said insistently, jerking the box away. "I can take care of him."

"Okay, forget I mentioned it. Grab that Fuzz Buster and we'll call it a day."

Elliott added it to the box as Michael turned out the light.

Upstairs E.T. was hard at work in the closet.

A definite machine was starting to take shape. A wooden coat hanger now served as a host for twenty-six colored wires, all of them attached to the open Speak & Spell. The speakers from the walkie-talkies were attached with duct tape to the front of the toy, and a heavy piece of video cable led from the speakers to the metal coffee can.

E.T. used his long, delicate fingers to explore the insides of what was once Gertie's Little Miss Moppet record player. The player was helpful, but he still needed more.

Elliott opened the closet door and put down the cardboard box from the garage. E.T.

looked up, and the boy could see that Michael had been speaking truthfully. He *did* look pale and sweaty, whereas before his skin had been dry and cool.

E.T. shivered. Elliott tried not to notice and began to empty the box. His mind more on the alien than on his task, he wasn't paying attention when he cut his finger on the ragged-toothed saw blade.

"Ouch!" Elliott said, pulling his forefinger back and blowing on the wound. A drop of bright blood welled out from the cut.

E.T. raised his own forefinger, and it slowly began to take on a brilliant orange glow, as if an ember of fire was embedded within the creature's fingertip.

Elliott's eyes widened as E.T. reached out with his glowing finger and touched the cut, gently pulling his fingertip down and across Elliott's injured hand. The orange glow faded. Elliott raised his cut finger. No more blood. No more pain. The injury had been healed instantly by E.T.'s touch.

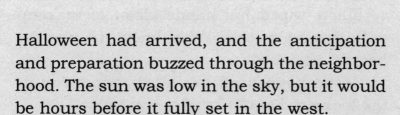

CHAPTER 13

Halloween had arrived, and the anticipation and preparation buzzed through the neighborhood. The sun was low in the sky, but it would be hours before it fully set in the west.

Gertie, dressed in her cowgirl outfit, watched as Elliott applied the last touches of his green monster makeup. Elliott eyed himself in the bathroom mirror. The makeup was a bit blotchy, and the more he fiddled with trying to smooth it, the lumpier it became.

"What do you think?" he asked. Gertie, standing on a stool so she could watch the application process, gave him an "okay" sign. Elliott decided that monsters probably didn't have smooth skin anyway, as he gooped on lots more of the sloppy green goo.

"No, and that is final!" Mary proclaimed loudly from her bedroom. "You are *not* going as a terrorist and that's final!"

"But, Mom, all the guys are," Michael replied, walking past the bathroom door.

Elliott turned and looked at Gertie. "You're going as a ghost," he said. "You promised."

Gertie tipped her hat back. "I know. I'm only pretending I'm going as a cowgirl."

Elliott wiped his hands clean of makeup onto the guest towel. "You know the plan by heart?" he asked.

Gertie hopped off her stool. "Meet you at the lookout. I'm not stupid, you know."

"Listen, buster, you won't get four blocks in this neighborhood dressed like a terrorist," Mary called, still laying down the law to Michael.

"Please?" Michael pleaded.

Mary was firm. "No."

"Fine! Fine! I'll just be a hobo again," Michael said, stomping past the bathroom door. Elliott grinned. Michael was already in his hobo costume, which indicated he knew he wouldn't win the terrorist debate.

Michael looked at his brother and sister and said, "Time to hit the road."

"Then let's finish suiting up," Elliott said.

The trio went into Elliott's bedroom and opened the closet door.

"Eeeeee!" E.T. screamed, gaping at Elliott's monster makeup.

"It's okay. It's only a costume. See?" Elliott said, smearing some of the green makeup off his cheek to show E.T. it was fake. "Are you ready?"

E.T. nodded. "Ready," he said softly.

Reaching down past the creature, Michael lifted a large box. The device E.T. had been building was finished. He hoisted it onto Elliott's back and strapped the gadget into place. Then he draped a cloak over Elliott's back and turned him into a perfectly service-able hunchbacked monster.

"Cool," Michael said.

"One last costume to go," said Elliott.

Mary, dressed in a leopard-print outfit and cat mask, sat on the sofa and covered her eyes, waiting for the parade of costumes.

"Okay, Mom, you can look now," Michael announced.

Mary opened her eyes.

First there was Elliott, the hideous green monster. Then there was Michael, a murdered old hobo. In a final gruesome gesture, Michael had attached a fake rubber knife on his neck and added streaks of fake blood.

"Gertie" stood between the boys as a short white ghost. But the figure beneath the sheet was really E.T. The height and shape beneath the sheet was about right, so long as Mary didn't look down and get a good look at the creature's feet.

Mary lifted her hands to her face with delight. "Don't move!" she said, hopping up and running into the dining room. Michael and Elliott exchanged nervous looks.

Trying to see through the eyeholes in the sheet, E.T. peered up and spotted Michael as well as the fake knife and blood on his neck.

"Ouch," E.T. whispered.

A red light began to glow under the sheet, and before anyone could stop him, he raised his healing finger to Michael's artificial wound.

"Stop! It's not real," Michael hissed. Elliott grabbed E.T.'s hand and shoved it back under the sheet, just as Mary returned with the Polaroid camera.

"You all look great!" Mary said, peering through the viewfinder.

"Thank you," Michael said.

"Thank you," Elliott said.

"Thank you," E.T. added.

Michael and Elliott both winced, but since Mary chose that moment to press the button of her camera, the sound covered up E.T.'s voice. When the flash went off, however, E.T.'s large, sensitive eyes were not prepared, and the power of the bright light shocked him.

His legs buckled as Michael and Elliott struggled to hold him up. Luckily, Mary paid no mind as she fiddled with the camera.

"Now, you guys stick with your sister—"

"Right," Michael said, inching toward the front door.

"You can go act crazy after you bring her back home."

"Not a problem, Mom," Elliott agreed.

Mary placed the photo on the coffee table and picked up her costume's magic wand.

"And don't go past the 7-Eleven, and don't eat anything that isn't wrapped, and—"

Michael rolled his eyes. "Don't eat any apples 'cause they may have razor blades and drink any punch 'cause it may have LSD in it."

"Hush, Michael," Mary said, shaking her wand at him. She bent over E.T. and kissed him on the nose through the sheet. Elliott's heart stopped.

"Er, Mom . . . would you fix this?" he said, trying to distract her attention away from E.T.

Mary stood and tied Elliott's cloak tight under his chin. "So, you're a hunchback?"

"A goblin," Elliott corrected as Michael opened the front door.

Elliott took one hand and Michael the other, and with E.T. between them, they led him down the driveway.

"And be home one hour after sundown. No later!" Mary called.

E.T. looked back at Mary, as if wanting a last bit of reassurance. Mary obliged, waving her magic wand at the small ghost.

Michael and Elliott hurried E.T. along, but he couldn't help gawking at the costumed humans walking past. For his first view of "earthling society," the boys could not have chosen to take E.T. out on a more unusual night.

Still, even with the sheet blocking most of his vision, E.T. saw enough to keep him continually distracted. The boys turned down an unpaved side street and began to head up a hill to the edge of the woods. The groups of trick-or-treaters thinned as they headed for the woods, and soon they were alone.

When they reached the fire road, they found Gertie, waiting for them in her cowgirl clothing with Elliott's bike. An umbrella was strapped to the rear of the bicycle, along with another small bag in the bike's handlebar basket.

They removed E.T.'s sheet and plopped it over Gertie's head. Wrapping the alien in a blanket, except for his eyes and face, Elliott and Michael lifted him into the bicycle's basket.

"I'll stall Mom as long as I can," Michael said. "But you've got to hurry."

Elliott nodded. Then he got onto the bike

and began to pedal it up the dirt road. Gertie and Michael watched as Elliott and E.T. rode away before they turned and headed back down into the twinkling lights and colorful costumes of their neighborhood.

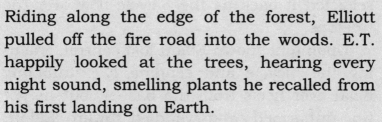

CHAPTER 14

Riding along the edge of the forest, Elliott pulled off the fire road into the woods. E.T. happily looked at the trees, hearing every night sound, smelling plants he recalled from his first landing on Earth.

"Elliott," E.T. said.

"Yes, E.T.?" Elliott gasped, huffing and puffing as he pedaled.

"E.T. phone home," he rasped, almost jumping up and down in his basket with excitement. "E.T. phone home!"

"Yes?" Elliott agreed, slowing down. "Here?"

"Come," E.T. said, pointing out farther, gesturing toward the heart of the forest.

Elliott slowed the speed of his pedaling.

"It's too bumpy. We'll have to walk from here."

But E.T. had another idea. As the bicycle bounced along, the creature closed his eyes, and the bicycle lifted into the air. Elliott gulped, grabbing the handlebars as his feet kept on pedaling. The bike rose up, up, up—silhouetting against the full moon as it arched effortlessly across the sky.

"Not too high, not too high!" Elliott squealed, laughing with joy.

The creature felt Elliott's excitement and reflected it back as the bicycle flew over the treetops.

Upon touchdown Elliott lost control, crashing the bicycle and sending E.T. tumbling head over heels from the basket, but he got up, unharmed, and waddled toward Elliott, who sat on the ground laughing. When Elliott calmed down, he took off his cape, and E.T. helped him unload the communicator.

Together, boy and alien placed the device on the ground, unfolding it for operation. The Speak & Spell was attached by simple, coated wires to a record player. The saw blade that had cut Elliott's finger rested on the turntable of the record player. The wooden hanger was positioned above the saw blade, and twenty-six colored wires protruded down to a fork. The fork moved along, one click at a time, in the teeth of the blade. A rope of colored wires led from the walkie-talkie speakers to the coffee can, which now housed a UHF receiver, scavenged from Mary's windowsill radio.

E.T. tied a string to the device, then stepped down a rock incline and moved into the forest. Elliott followed him and helped E.T. tie the other end of the string to a tree limb that swayed in the wind. Then Elliott raced back to the landing site and peered down at the active communicator.

The surface of the Speak & Spell lit up, and on the tiny digital screen were dots, dashes . . . alien shapes for an unknown language. Faint musical sounds emanated from the walkie-talkie speakers.

E.T. stepped up beside Elliott and pointed to a spool of wire. The creature then took the wire in his long hands and slid the naked copper end into the vein of a tree leaf. He dug another snip of wire into the trunk of a massive redwood. The alien collected the wires, tying them into a single strand . . . tapping the very life force of the forest into his plea to home.

Together, Elliott and E.T. stood looking up at the night sky, waiting.

Mary sat on the bottom step of the front porch, an empty candy bowl beside her as she twirled her magic wand. Even with most of her expression hidden behind her cat mask, it was plain that she was angry and worried.

The boys and Gertie were late. The sun had set hours ago. Standing up with a sigh, she reached inside the front door for her purse and keys and headed for the car. After she drove down the driveway and vanished into the night, a lone figure stepped out of the shadows, climbing the walk to their front door. A hand reached down and tested the knob. The door swung open easily, the night wind blowing out the candle of a lone jack-o'-lantern on the landing.

The man stepped into the room, walking briskly, keys jingling at his waist. He took a small Geiger counter from a pack on his back and began to wave it around, looking for evidence of . . . well, of what exactly, he wasn't sure.

The Geiger counter began to click as he followed the sounds to Elliott's room. The counter clicked rapidly as he pushed open the closet door to reveal E.T.'s nesting place. The man knelt down and picked up a stray bit of wire left behind from the creature's building of the communicator. He held it up and looked intently at it, pondering the possibilities.

Mary felt her blood pressure rise. There they were, a stubby ghost and a lanky hobo, both innocently walking down the sidewalk as if they didn't have a care in the world. She pulled up to the street corner and rolled down her window.

"Get. In. The Car," she said tightly. "Now."

Michael and Gertie did as they were told.

"Now, where's Elliott?"

Silence.

"I'm asking you a question."

Gertie peered up at Michael, pulling the

sheet off her head. "What I wanna know is why *would* Elliott go to the forest anyway? It's dark."

Mary peered at Michael in the rearview mirror. Michael shrugged and tried to smile.

CHAPTER 15

Elliott helped E.T. open the umbrella, revealing the interior covered in aluminum foil. They attached the handle of the umbrella to the coffee can and UHF receiver. E.T. connected even more wires to the can and then stepped back to examine his work. The wind blew. The communicator moved and sent invisible beams upward to the sky.

"We have to go now," Elliott whispered. "We're so late already."

E.T. was silent, listening to the communicator, feeling the wind.

"We have to go home, E.T." Elliott pleaded.

The creature's head dropped, his chin hitting his chest. "Home."

"You need to give them some time," Elliott said, sitting next to his friend. E.T. looked over, his wide, kind eyes filled with tears. He placed his hand on his chest.

"Ouch," E.T. whispered.

Elliott began to cry. "You could be happy here," he said. "I'd take care of you. I wouldn't let anybody hurt you."

E.T. didn't answer. He sat and looked at the sky. Elliott stayed beside him, waiting for something to arrive and help them, but the sky remained the same.

At dawn Elliott awoke with a shudder, damp from morning dew. He rolled over to find he was alone with the broadcasting communicator, now silent. As Elliott struggled to get to his feet, he was a bit surprised to find himself so weak and cold. His goblin makeup had smeared down his face with sleep and tears, and his eyes were bloodshot.

He was alone.

"E.T.?" he called out, panicked, but there was no answer.

Inside her kitchen Mary paced, wiping the counter clean for the sixtieth time as she spoke to a uniformed police officer sitting at the table. The officer wrote something in his notebook, then looked to her again for more details.

"I guess he's about four foot eight, you know, a small person. He was . . ."—her voice caught in her throat—"He was dressed as a hunchback."

"Was there any indication that he might have run away?" the officer asked. "Any family problems or recent arguments?"

"Well, my husband and I were recently separated, and it hasn't been easy on the kids," Mary explained.

"My father is in Mexico," Gertie volunteered, sitting with Michael on the sofa in the playroom across from the kitchen. They were still in their costumes, neither of them having slept during the long night.

Hoping to sneak in unnoticed, Elliott slowly walked into the kitchen from the back door.

"Elliott!" Mary called, racing over and hugging him tight.

The policeman flipped his notebook shut. "Is this our missing person?" he asked gently.

"Yes! Yes," Mary said, turning and taking the officer's hand. "Oh, thank you. He's back."

Michael and Gertie huddled in close as Mary saw the policeman out.

"Is E.T. here?" Elliott whispered. Michael shook his head "no."

Mary stepped back into the kitchen and placed a hand on Elliott's forehead. "Oh, Elliott. You're so cold," she said. "You're chilled from spending the night outside."

"I'm sorry," Elliott said meekly.

"Don't you ever do this again!" Mary replied, and held his face tight. Then she patted Gertie on the shoulder. "Go upstairs and draw your brother a hot bath."

Gertie left to draw the bath as Mary looked in the refrigerator for something to give Elliott to drink.

"You've got to find him, Mike," Elliott whispered, pleading. "He's somewhere in the forest near the bald spot."

Michael nodded, slipping out as Mary came

over with a cup of cool water. Outside the door Michael found Elliott's bicycle and hopped on, careening down the driveway and pedaling as fast as he could for the forest. He hoped his mother was too engrossed in Elliott's return to notice his absence until he could make it back.

Across the way, at the edge of the cul-de-sac, Michael glanced behind him and spotted an unusual black car creeping along the side of the road. Michael turned left and so did the car. He took a new turn, and again he was followed.

A sick feeling crept across Michael's chest. Elliott had been right all along. E.T. wasn't safe. None of them were.

Thinking fast, he twisted the handlebars and cut through a backyard, heading into an alleyway behind some houses. The car took a side street, keeping the pace and staying close.

"Fine," Michael muttered as he rode the bike up a dirt embankment, pedaling in the opposite direction. "Try tailing me here!"

The car squealed to a stop, stranded, watching as Michael blazed a new path, heading for the forest.

"E.T." he called out. He spotted the abandoned communicator, the umbrella now blown over, the strings still pulling in the wind as the signal beamed outward.

The distinct *chop chop chop* of a helicopter floated through the morning air. Michael peered up, ducking under the sheltering-canopy of a tree. The craft flew past the area, and he stepped out, a feeling of hopelessness flooding his entire body.

Looking at the communicator, he began to walk in a widening circle, searching for signs of E.T. He wondered for a moment if, perhaps, the plan had proven successful, and E.T. had signaled his home. If that were the case, the creature might already be a galaxy away.

But Elliott had seemed awfully sure that E.T. was still here, and in matters regarding the alien, Michael trusted his brother's instincts. He struggled to calm himself and pushed the bike along the bumpier sections of the forest floor, grateful to spot another trail leading down to the stream below. He rode slowly along the edge of the ridge above the winding waterway, and then he saw a flash of white below.

"No," he whispered.

E.T. was lying in the water on his side, his neck and head twisted at a grotesque angle. He was still, his body nearly as pale as snow, not the dark brown it usually was. The blanket Elliott had wrapped him in lay tangled at the edge of the stream. E.T. must have lost his balance and tumbled down into the shallow part of the water.

Michael grabbed the blanket and slid down the embankment, trying to keep his balance. A raccoon wandered near E.T., sniffing, until Michael shouted and scared the animal away.

Michael stooped down and gently lifted E.T.'s head, resting his hand against the creature's chest. E.T. was breathing, but barely, the air going in and out as a raspy wheeze. Michael pulled E.T. from the water and covered him with the blanket.

The sounds of the helicopter returned above him, and Michael glared up at the sky, his knees shaking as he carried his blanketed bundle. He managed to balance E.T. in the basket, and rode away wobbly, vanishing once more under the cover of the green trees.

CHAPTER 16

Mary had placed Elliott in the master bedroom. He was flat on his back, and staring at the ceiling. She stepped inside with a bowl of soup for him and a mug of coffee for herself. She held out a spoonful of the tomato soup to Elliott, but he shook his head "no." Mary placed the bowl on the nightstand, then sat down and placed an arm around Elliott's shoulders.

"Can't you tell me what's the matter?"

"I feel like everything is worth nothing," Elliott said.

Mary hugged him. "Oh, baby," she said. "That's no way to feel."

"I try to do the right thing, and I just make

everything worse," Elliott whispered.

"Everyone feels like that sometimes," Mary assured him. "You can only do the best you can do."

Elliott closed his eyes and drifted off. Soon the exhausted Mary was asleep as well. But Elliott slept lightly, and he heard the clatter from below as Michael struggled to make his way up the stairs with E.T. Elliott waited a few minutes, then slid carefully out of bed and walked over to his bedroom door. Michael motioned for Elliott to join him.

Inside Elliott's closet E.T. sat in his nesting area, wrapped in a heavy quilt. His skin was still pale. His large eyes opened sleepily as Elliott and Michael sat on either side of him. Elliott took E.T.'s hand and shivered at how cold the creature's body now felt.

"We've got to do something," Michael said. "Maybe Mom can—"

"We can't tell," Elliott insisted.

Michael spoke in a loud whisper. "Men followed me, Elliott! Aren't you listening? Why would anyone follow me unless they already knew?"

"We can only do the best we can do!" Elliott

said. "We'll lose him if we tell."

E.T. turned and looked at Michael.

"We'll lose him if we *don't* tell," he said. "And, Elliott, we'll lose you, too."

Elliott lifted E.T.'s long forefinger and touched it to the creature's chest.

"Heal yourself. Can't you?"

"No," E.T. said slowly.

"We've got to warm him up somehow," Michael decided. "Let's take him into the bathroom. Put him in the tub."

Elliott nodded, helping his older brother as they struggled to move the alien out of the closet. E.T. tried to help, but he was terribly weak. Elliott staggered, his own weakness matching that of the creature.

Michael managed to herd them both into the bathroom and tub, but was scared to run any water. Elliott, cradling E.T., was now as pale as he was. The alien's eyes were closed.

Michael sighed and walked out of the bathroom into Mary's bedroom.

"Mom," he said.

Mary snapped to attention from her dozing. "Where's Elliott?" she asked, getting to her feet and picking up her mug of coffee.

Michael backed away, out of the door and into the hall. "Mom, I have something really serious to tell you."

"Is he gone again?" Mary asked, her voice rising in pitch as she pushed past Michael.

"But first you've got to promise," Michael continued.

Mary turned and looked at him. "What is it?" she asked.

"Come with me," Michael said, turning and leading her toward the bathroom. Mary followed, gripping the mug, a sense of dread filling her body.

Michael stopped at the bathroom door. "Mom? Do you remember that goblin?"

"What are you talking about?"

"Mom, I need you to make a promise," he said. "Just swear to the most excellent promise you can make."

"Michael!" Mary said, annoyed now.

Michael opened the door to the bathroom. Gertie was sitting on the counter, still in cowgirl attire, swinging her legs. Mary gave her a smile, then turned her attention to the area of the bathroom next to the tub where Gertie was so intently looking.

Elliott was now sitting on the floor. Mary felt relief wash over her body, and she stepped inside . . . peering past Elliott and seeing E.T. at last.

Only, this was not the vibrant, glowing E.T. of days past. This E.T. was a chalky white, his skin peeling. The creature saw Mary and weakly extended his arms.

A stunned Mary did not speak. The mug slid from her hands, shattering on the floor, sending ceramic shards and coffee droplets everywhere.

"He's sick," Elliott said softly. "*We're* sick. I think we're dying."

Mary covered her mouth with her hands.

"Mom, he won't hurt us—"

"Michael, take Gertie downstairs. *Now*," Mary commanded as she reached down and scooped Elliott up from the coffee-stained tile floor.

"He's the man from the moon, Mama," Gertie wailed as Michael took her piggyback down the stairs. Mary followed, Elliott in her arms, his head peering over her shoulder and back at the pale, moaning E.T.

"We can't leave him alone," Elliott whispered as Mary strode out of the bathroom, heading down the stairs behind Michael.

"Start the car," she called as Michael flung open the front door to find an astronaut.

He backed away, stunned. Mary gaped, then reached out and slammed the door shut. The door reopened and the astronaut stepped inside, his breathing hollow and labored from within the suit. Michael turned and tried to run into the playroom, and promptly found himself dodging the arms of a second space-suit-wearing intruder already in the house.

Gertie screamed as the family jostled past and found the way out blocked by another astronaut. Helpless, everyone backed up together in a corner, seeing more men in space suits stepping inside. One of them was taping heavy plastic over the windows. Another draped the furniture.

Mary took all of this in and then shouted out, "You can't do this! This is my home!"

The men did not answer.

Outside, as the sun began to rise in the sky, a line of men wearing helmets and blue "hazardous materials" suits marched up the street toward Mary's house. All around them in the cul-de-sac were vans, police cars, and other vehicles pulled into a lineup, blocking off the area.

From rooftop to ground the house was draped in a heavy, transparent plastic. Huge air hoses climbed up over the roof and circled the perimeter of the structure. Bright lights, braced on tall scaffolding, illuminated the home. Trailers and trucks blocked off the driveway, and more men helped push a large plastic tunnel up the driveway and into place at the front door.

One of the men in space suits entered the bathroom inside the quarantined area.

E.T., his skin now gone from white to gray, lay on his back.

"Home," E.T. whispered helplessly.

CHAPTER 17

A man in a light blue protective jumpsuit walked up to the chaotic scene at the house. A ring of keys jingled at his hip. He pulled on a white pair of plastic gloves and a breathing hood, and stepped through the long plastic tunnel that led into the house.

His friendly but concerned face was under-lit by a white light inside the hood. His hair was mussed across his furrowed forehead, giving him a studious, boyish air as he hurried through the tunnel.

In just the last hour the house had been invaded by physicians and psychiatrists, biologists and geologists, radiologists and cardiologists . . . anyone and everyone that could assist in helping Elliott, and the alien visitor, recover from the ailment that was plaguing them.

And once the alien had recovered, then the secrets of the creature would be unlocked and shared with the world.

Mary stood in the middle of the room, Gertie at her side. A doctor took a blood sample from her arm while another questioned her about E.T.

"Let me go to my son," Mary said wearily.

"Have any environmental changes occurred since the, ah . . . creature has been sequestered in your home?" the doctor asked. "Temperature? Humidity? Light intensity?"

Another physician took Michael's blood pressure while a nurse clipped a lock of Gertie's hair for analysis. "Son," the physician asked, "did you notice any superficial changes in his skin color or breathing? Any hair loss, any evidence of surface sweating?"

"He never had any hair," Michael said, drained of energy.

"Apparently they've been able to establish a primitive language system with the creature. Seven, eight words," said another doctor.

One of the men turned to Gertie and asked, "Have you seen your friend exhibit any emotions? Has he laughed or cried?"

Gertie bit her lower lip. "Elliott said he cried," she said softly.

The man with the keys looked up at an observation monitor showing Elliott and E.T. lying on hospital beds in what was once the playroom, but was now a plastic-encased hospital ward.

"How does he communicate?" he asked Michael.

"He communicates through Elliott," Michael explained.

"Elliott thinks his thoughts?"

"No," Michael paused for a moment. "Elliott feels his feelings," he corrected.

The man with the keys walked toward the playroom. It pulsed with electronic equipment, monitors, and machinery, all of it beeping and clicking softly, mixing with the urgent conversation going on around it.

While Elliott was being cared for, most of the attention of the physicians was on E.T. Both of them lay on hospital beds in a portable "clean room," encased in germ-free plastic.

"I'm getting a reading now, not a human EKG pattern."

"Have you got a location on his heart and thorax?"

"I don't know."

The doctors had their arms inserted into the clean room via long rubber sleeves with gloves at the ends. Both boy and alien were pale, and even in the cool air they were sweating profusely.

"I'm running the sonar over the creature's thorax now."

"Location?"

"Per human."

"Heart?"

"Difficult to see."

"Does he have a heart?" a nurse wondered.

"The whole screen is lit up. It looks like his whole chest is a heart."

The clean room was unzipped and two doctors, followed by the man with the keys, entered. The physicians split, one attending E.T., the other Elliott.

"You're scaring him," Elliott whispered, his voice faint and sick.

The key man stepped forward, looking

down at Elliott. "Can you tell him not to be scared?" he asked gently.

"Leave him alone, leave him alone," Elliott moaned, looking up into the man's face. "I can take care of him."

"Elliott," the man said firmly. "I've been to the forest. I saw your machine. What does it do, Elliott?"

"It's a communicator," Elliott replied, his voice barely audible. "Is it still working?"

"Yes," the man said.

"He came to me, he came to me for help," Elliott said, trying to explain even as his body temperature continued to rise.

"He came to me, too," the man replied, reaching down and taking Elliott's hand. "I've been wishing for this, Elliott. I've been wishing for this since I was ten years old. I don't want him to die."

Elliott turned, looking over at E.T. "He wants to stay with me. He doesn't know you."

"Elliott, your friend is a rare and valuable creature. We want to know him. If we get to know him, we can learn so many things about the universe, and about life. You understand that, don't you?"

Elliott turned back to him and nodded.

"And it's because of you that we might all get to finally know something about ourselves. Because you saved E.T. and protected him and were good to him. Can you let us do our part now? Can you let us try to save him?"

"He . . . was calling his people on the communicator," Elliott said. "He was calling them."

Another doctor peered through the plastic. "Blood pressure is dropping."

"Why was he calling them, Elliott? What's wrong with him?"

"He wants to go home."

One of the doctors checked a monitor. "E.T.'s condition is worsening, but Elliott's is stabilizing."

Elliott turned to look at the creature again. "E.T.?"

E.T. rolled his head over and looked at Elliott. The creature's wide eyes were near slits now. He took a labored breath and spoke: "Elliott."

"You can stay with me," Elliott said. "I'll be right here."

"Stay, stay," E.T. echoed, turning his head away and closing his eyes.

A nurse checked a monitor screen. "The boy is coming back," she said, her voice tight. "But we're losing E.T."

Upstairs Michael stepped into Elliott's bedroom, which was eerily quiet. He went inside the closet, flicking on the lamp to look at the nesting area where E.T. had stayed.

Tools lay on the floor, along with books and toys. The page of comic strips from the newspaper was folded to the *Flash Gordon* daily, showing the communicator in action. Michael sat down among the items, resting his back against the cushioning where E.T. had leaned. Hot tears fell down his cheeks as he spied the geranium Gertie had given E.T.

Suddenly the plant began to sink into the dirt, and the stems drooped and wilted. The petals of the flowers dried up and fell off in a yellow rain. Michael grabbed the plant as a horrifying realization washed over him. "No!" he screamed.

In the playroom Elliott also screamed, "Don't go, E.T.! Don't go!"

Mary and Gertie were now there, watching the scene from behind the protective plastic wall as the doctor worked frantically, trying to revive the dying creature. Overhead E.T.'s heart monitor was flat-lining.

"There's no blood pressure, no pulse."

"Should I prepare CPR, doctor?"

"I don't know . . . try shocking him."

"Leave him alone! You're killing him!" Elliott protested, even as the man with the keys lifted him up and carried him over to Mary's waiting arms.

The electric paddles were applied to try and start E.T.'s heart again. "Clear!" the attendant called.

E.T.'s body jolted from the electricity, but his heart remained still. Gertie winced, watching the scene as tears streaked her face. The heart-rate line ran flat along the monitor screen. Gertie held her doll tight.

"Again!" the doctor said, and another jolt was unleashed.

"No response," a nurse said.

Michael ran into the room, clutching the dead geranium, already knowing what he would find. He joined his family, and they looked on in somber silence as the doctors stepped back from E.T.'s lifeless body.

The key man looked down at E.T., then turned away as a nurse reached up and turned off the steady drone of the emergency alarm, leaving nothing but the sound of a grief-stricken Elliott's sobbing.

CHAPTER 18

There was a flurry of activity at the end of the street. Doctors in blue jumpsuits, uniformed policemen, and even military personnel began to break down the plastic quarantine around Elliott's house.

"Something's happening," Steve announced. He was on his bike behind one of the saw-horses that blocked off the cul-de-sac. Tyler and Greg, also straddling their bikes, agreed. Most of the neighborhood had flocked here, either out of worry or curiosity.

"Man, what I wouldn't give to be inside Mike's house right now," Tyler agreed. "I'll bet something awesome is going on . . ."

Unfortunately, the mood inside the house

was not one of jubilation. The medical staff, having realized their efforts to revive E.T. were fruitless, packed up their equipment.

An order came down from Washington: Place the alien on ice for preservation, then transport it. One by one the adults stepped away from the body, their attentions drawn elsewhere, their own emotions at the loss of the creature racing through their minds. Elliott stood vigil over his friend as Mary, Gertie, and Michael hovered in the background.

No one spoke. There was nothing to say.

The key man walked into the room and pulled off his protective headgear. He knelt down next to Elliott and sighed.

"Is he dead?" Gertie finally asked.

"I think so," Mary said.

"I wish he were back," said Gertie.

Two attendants rolled in a silver metal casing filled with ice to preserve E.T. for his journey across the country. Mary picked up Gertie and left the room.

"They're going to take him now, Elliott," the man said gently, standing and placing a hand on Elliott's shoulder as they watched the men place E.T. inside a zippered plastic bag, and then in the bottom of his silver coffin. They carefully closed the lid, which locked into place with a soft hiss. The clear oval canopy of the cylinder clouded over with condensation, obscuring the sight of the body within.

"They're just going to cut him all up," Elliott said softly, images of biology class passing through his mind.

"Do you want to spend some time alone with him?" he asked.

Elliott nodded, and the key man gave a sign to the technicians. The adults walked out of the room, past Michael, who lingered for a second, and then also left his brother in his grief. Soon the room was empty except for Elliott, who stared down, his voice choking as he tried to speak.

"Look at what they've done to you," he whispered. "I'm so sorry. You must be dead because I-I don't know how to feel. I can't feel anything anymore."

Elliott ran his hand along the casing of the cylinder.

"You've gone someplace else now, E.T.,"

Elliott said, his voice breaking as he turned and walked away from the lifeless body. "I love you, E.T."

A red light began to pulsate from within the casing, but Elliott didn't notice.

On the countertop, placed there by Michael, sat the wilted pot of geraniums. Elliott sniffed, wiping his eyes as he looked at the flowers.

Was it his imagination, or had one of the buds just moved?

The boy gaped as the stems straightened and the flower petals burst forth into a vibrant yellow. He spun around and ran back to the cylinder. A red glow shined through the transparent canopy as he unlocked the lid and threw it open.

E.T.'s heart-light was shining. He was alive!

Elliott unzipped the plastic bag, and E.T.'s head and face popped into view.

"E.T. phone home!" the creature announced triumphantly.

Elliott screamed with joy.

"Home, home, home, home," sang E.T., sharing in Elliott's delight.

"Does this mean they're coming?" Elliott

asked, his eyes darting skyward.

"Yes!" E.T. said firmly. "Home! Home!"

Elliott looked around. They were still alone, but not for long.

"Look, you've got to stay here," Elliott said, pushing E.T. back down into the transport cylinder. "If they see you—"

"Home!"

"You gotta shut up, already," Elliott said, quickly shutting the lid on the babbling E.T. at the same instant that the man with the keys returned with the attendants.

Elliott draped his body over the oval shape to cover E.T.'s heart-light and pretended to cry. The man pulled Elliott away as the technicians rolled the silver cylinder out of the room. The clear portal of the canopy was frosted once more from the dry ice within.

Elliott spotted Michael out in the hallway. He waved him over, then pointed to the pot of geraniums, which were continuing to grow and bloom.

"He's alive," Elliott whispered.

A wide smile broke across Michael's face. "Where is he?"

Elliott turned and pointed to the men with

the cylinder. The boys followed the attendants, who walked up one of the plastic tun-
nels. The tunnel ended outside the house,
where it was attached to the open back doors
of a waiting white van. E.T. was placed inside
and then they stepped out.

Michael and Elliott looked at each other.

"I've got a plan," Elliott said.

Moments later Gertie skipped up to Mary,
carrying the pot of blooming geraniums. She
also had a piece of folded notebook paper. The
key man stood with Mary, discussing Elliott.
Gertie listened for a moment, but quickly grew
bored and started to fidget.

"Mama?" she asked, tugging the hem of
Mary's blouse.

Mary looked down.

"Mama," Gertie continued. "Are they gone
yet?"

"Is who gone, honey?"

"Michael and Elliott," Gertie replied, holding
up the sheet of paper. "I'm supposed to give
you this note when they're gone."

"Excuse me," Mary said, stepping away from the man, and she reached down to Gertie. "Give it to me now, Gertie."

Gertie handed over the piece of paper. Mary sat down on the staircase and began to read. "Oh, my god," she said as her eyes scanned the page.

Elliott walked briskly down the tunnel, trying to look sad. He passed two men dressed in the blue jumpsuits. He then glanced back to make sure he wasn't being followed and ran the rest of the way to the transport van.

He hopped in and crawled past the cylinder with E.T. inside, making his way to the front seat.

"About time," Michael said, shifting nervously behind the steering wheel. Michael had swiped one of the official blue jumpsuits, but had neglected to add the face hood.

"Where's your mask?" Elliott demanded.

"Uh—"

A uniformed police officer walked past the

van, did a double take, and backed up to eyeball Michael. He rapped on the window.

"Who are you?" he demanded.

Michael smiled and gave him a thumbs-up. "I'm the driver," he said, turning the ignition key on. The van's engine came to life. The officer responded by taking out his walkie-talkie and calling hurriedly for backup. "Open this door," he demanded.

Michael looked back at Elliott helplessly.

"What are you waiting for? Floor it!" Elliott yelled, looking back into the plastic tunnel attached to the rear doors of the van and seeing a group of the masked men in jumpsuits running toward him.

Michael floored it, and the van lurched forward, careening across the front yard away from the house as the teenager struggled to gain control of the vehicle. The plastic tunnel tore away from the van with a loud, ripping sound.

"I've never driven forward before!" he cried as he ran over the family mailbox and dodged a parked fire truck. Until now, Michael had only practiced backing his mother's car out of the garage.

Spotting his friends on their bicycles, Michael slowed down long enough to scream at them, "Meet us at the playground at the top of the hill. And bring our bikes!"

CHAPTER 19

The trio of boys snagged the needed extra bicycles from Mary's garage before pedaling against the onrush of vehicles already in pursuit of Michael and Elliott. The gang turned off the cul-de-sac and took a series of backyard shortcuts toward the playground.

Mary backed out of the garage at sixty miles per hour. Gertie was buckled in next to her, holding the pot of blooming geraniums in her lap.

The key man ran up to the driver's-side window. "Where are you going?" he demanded.

"To the spaceship!" Gertie blurted out. Mary shot her a dirty look as realization dawned on the man's face.

"I'm coming with you," he said, climbing into the backseat.

"Be careful, would you?" Elliott told Michael as the van lurched, tossing E.T.'s silver cylinder to the floor. The cylinder sprung open, flooding the rear compartment with a dry ice haze and the color red as E.T.'s heartlight pulsated.

"Home!" E.T. said.

Michael regained control of the steering wheel. "We're gonna die, and they're never going to give me my license," he moaned.

He took the van around the corner, swerving past a series of dark government sedans and wailing police cars that had taken an alternate route in pursuit. The police cars were in turn followed by Mary's car.

"Where is the park anyway?" Michael called.

"Near the 7-Eleven," Elliott replied, poking

his head back through the curtains and looking through the windshield.

"Where's that?"

"I don't know the streets!" Elliott said helplessly. "Mom always drives me!"

"Never mind. I think I got it," Michael said, turning the wheel sharp and roaring up over a sidewalk onto the green grass of the neighborhood park. In the distance behind them, a group of police cars approached, their sirens blaring.

Michael steered the van between a seesaw and a swing set, hit the brakes, and brought the van to a stop near his friends. Elliott had opened the rear doors of the van, and a foglike haze wafted out from the dry ice that had been intended to preserve E.T.'s body.

The other boys and Michael ran around to the back of the van. Waiting calmly for them were Elliott and E.T., whose heart-light flashed red through the dry ice vapor.

Elliott hopped down and looked at the older boys. "Okay, he's a man from outer space and we're taking him to his spaceship," he told them matter-of-factly.

"W-Why can't he just beam up?" a

nervous, dumbfounded Greg asked.

Elliott looked at Greg and rolled his eyes. "This is reality, Greg."

"We've got to go," Michael said as he picked up Elliott's bike. "Where to?"

"The forest," Elliott said, picking up E.T. and placing him in the basket as he had done on Halloween. "It's a straight shot down the hill. Just follow me."

At the edge of the park a series of automobiles that included Mary's small car converged on the van. Officers leapt from their vehicles with their guns drawn and sprinted toward their destination.

Mary ran after them, holding Gertie as she screamed, "Don't shoot! They're only children!"

One of the officers flung open the back doors of the van. The interior was empty. The steel cylinder was open. The boys and the alien were now on bikes and moving.

And they were closer than anyone might have suspected. On a street three blocks over, the boys pedaled as fast as they could, two boys on either side of Elliott. E.T. was covered from prying eyes by a white blanket, but his wide eyes and face peered through his disguise as he gripped the sides of the basket.

Two cars came squealing in from a side street, but the bikers easily outmaneuvered them, cutting across a construction site. The muddy pathways littered with boards and brick were too treacherous for cars, but not for bikes!

A new car, tan in color with UNITED STATES GOVERNMENT written on the door, broke away from the pack of pursuers and skidded down another paved road, trying to outflank the kids by moving parallel and beating them to the bottom of the hill. Now all they had to do was wait for the kids to come to them. . . .

CHAPTER 20

As far as Elliott and the others could see, they had a free path to the forest. "Yeah! We made it!" Tyler cried, taking off his hat and waving it, narrowly missing being grabbed by a plain-clothes officer running beside him.

With the appearance of more on-foot pursuers, Tyler's joy of freedom was short lived. Up ahead, the tan car pulled across the street, blocking it. Other cars also appeared, creating a blockade.

Elliott and E.T. rode forward, the enemy at their heels.

"Look out!" Michael cried. "They've got guns!"

Indeed, their pursuers carried rifles and shotguns and leveled them at the group of bicycling boys as they hurtled ever closer to the roadblock.

Elliott's mind raced . . . We're going to have to stop, he thought.

E.T. didn't agree.

The creature closed his wide eyes, and like magic, the five bicycles rose into the air, easily clearing the roadblock and sailing above the trees lining the street.

The bikes flew in formation, hurtling over the rooftops of the neighborhood, as everyone but Elliott clutched their handlebars in a mix of terror and delight. Elliott had no fear. He embraced the thrill of the experience, drinking in the beauty of the world surrounding them as they flew across the setting sun.

"Awesome!" Elliott screamed with delight.

"Is this real? Is this really real?" Tyler asked, looking down at his feet on the pedals and at the ground far below.

Greg closed his eyes tight. "Tell me when it's over!" he said.

E.T. knew where he was going and steered the bikes to the right. The boys held on tight. The creature, whose strength had returned, effortlessly brought them down along the familiar path in the forest that led to the bald spot in the woods.

Elliott helped E.T. out of the basket, and together the pair went over to the communicator that E.T. had constructed. Elliott knelt, brushing away leaves from the turntable, and it began to rotate once more, tripping the fork along the surface of the saw blade.

Suddenly the woods filled with blue light.

Elliott and the others looked up at the sky as the ball-shaped spacecraft slowly descended. It was a magical sight to everyone, even E.T., who had seen the ship of light a countless number of times.

"Home," E.T. said, his red heart-light fluttering. As the ship landed, the blue light changed to a golden yellow, and shifted again into a glowing pastel purple. A ramp lowered itself from the entrance of the ship, as the great craft waited for the missing occupant to come on board.

Mary's car pulled up to the edge of the forest. "There they are!" squealed Gertie, and Mary stopped the car. Gertie ran from the automobile, the tall grass of the forest floor almost up to her neck.

She walked up to E.T and presented him with the potted geranium.

"I just wanted to say good-bye," she said.

Michael placed an arm around Gertie's shoulders. "He doesn't know good-bye," he told her.

E.T. held the geranium with one of his hands and reached out with the other to pat Gertie gently on the head. "Be . . . good," the creature told her.

"Yes," Gertie replied, kissing E.T. on the nose.

Michael placed a hand on E.T.'s head for a few seconds, his voice catching in his throat. He then stepped back as E.T. set the geranium on the ground.

Mary and the man were now at the edge of the scene, joining Greg, Steve, and Tyler. Michael picked up Gertie and stepped back to meet them, leaving Elliott to walk with E.T. to the edge of the ramp of the ship.

"Come?" E.T. asked.

"Stay," Elliott replied.

The two friends stared at each other for a moment, neither of them having to speak, communicating through their emotions. Then together, they reached their arms out and embraced.

Reluctantly E.T. broke the hug and touched his chest, where his heart-light was now a deep ruby glow that illuminated their faces.

"Ouch," E.T. said sadly.

Elliott took E.T.'s forefinger and pressed it to his own chest.

"Ouch," Elliott repeated.

E.T. moved the finger up to Elliott's forehead, touching it lightly. The tip glowed red.

"I'll be right here," E.T. said, tapping Elliott's temple.

Elliott nodded "yes" and began to cry a little as E.T. picked up his geranium and waddled up the ramp of the ship. Inside the doorway another being of E.T.'s kind appeared with a glowing red heart-light shining like a beacon to guide E.T.'s way into the spaceship.

"Bye," Elliott whispered as E.T. entered the ship, and the circular doorway closed shut. The ramp lifted up, sliding into a slot on the craft, and the ship began to rise into the air.

Above the watchers a shining globe of light

climbed higher and higher and then in an instant sped away, leaving behind a bright rainbow against the darkness.

Mary laughed with delight. She glanced over and spied the look of gratitude on the man's face at being allowed to witness the scene. Michael hugged Gertie, unashamed of feeling so happy.

As for Elliott, he gazed upward, his mind dreaming of the future—and of the day when he might be reunited with his friend.

He hoped it would be soon.

ABOUT THE AUTHOR

Terry Collins is the author of dozens of books for young readers. A former newspaper reporter and columnist, he's active today in theater arts, and he teaches acting when not clacking the keys of his typewriter. Terry lives in Mount Airy, North Carolina with his wife, Ginny. And on nights when the moon is full, he still looks skyward, hoping to see Elliott and E.T. fly by.

He dedicates this book to his grandfather James Vance Hutson.

BE AN *E.T.* TORCHBEARER.

2002 marks the 20th anniversary of E.T. The Extra-Terrestrial. During this time of celebration, E.T. will carry the torch for Special Olympics. Here are some ways you can help too...

 Be a friend to a person with mental disabilities. E.T. and Elliott didn't let differences stand in the way of friendship. Follow their example by spending time with someone with mental disabilities, learning about their challenges and what they like to do.

 Become a fan of a Special Olympics athlete or team. Cheer for Special Olympics athletes at local competitions. Make posters to hang at school to let everyone know that your friends will be going for the gold.

Rid the world of "Retard." Stop calling people "retard" and encourage your friends to stop saying that hurtful and disrespectful word.

 Label them Able. Everyone has different levels of abilities. Recognize people for what they can do, not for what they can't do.

Visit the E.T. 20th Anniversary Web site (www.et20.com) or the Special Olympics Web site (www.specialolympics.org) to learn more great things about the E.T.-Special Olympics partnership.